Celebrating What truly Matters

POWERS IRISH WHISKEY
SHORT STORY COLLECTION

VOLUME TWO

AN ANTHOLOGY OF SHORT STORIES BY VARIOUS AUTHORS

EDITOR
RÓISÍN INGLE, THE IRISH TIMES

ILLUSTRATIONS
IAN MCCAFFREY
WWW.STORYBOARDS.IE

COVER & BOOK DESIGN
MAEVE CHAPMAN, IRISH DISTILLERS PERNOD RICARD

ACKNOWLEDGEMENTS

A huge thank you to each individual author for their wonderful short stories, a creative generosity without which this collection would not have been possible.

A special thanks to all at the Irish Times, in particular Orna Mulcahy and Róisín Ingle for their invaluable contribution and advice.

A special tribute to Maeve Binchy, who sadly passed away in July 2012. Maeve who was an enthusiastic supporter of this collection wrote a wonderful introduction to accompany this book. One of Ireland's master storytellers, Maeve will remain an inspiration to future generations of Irish authors. May she rest in peace.

To all those involved in Celebrating What Truly Matters, thank you.

 **THE IRISH TIMES**
irishtimes.com

Introduction

MAEVE BINCHY

What we REALLY want is to love and be loved in return.

It doesn't sound at all cool to say this but basically that's it.

We may THINK that we want thinner thighs and an affluent lifestyle.

We may ache to be on a List.

The Lists differ: to be among the country's best dressed, or most successful business person, or sportspersons of the year or becoming an A list celebrity. We might want degrees, diplomas, the latest gadgets, the sleekest cars the recognition from head waiters in restaurants, designer clothes or to have a home like a show house.

All these are human expectations hopes and dreams and not necessarily selfish or trivial. It's how we live our lives. But underneath it all what we REALLY want is to have some meaning, to need and be needed, to know the security of love.

Right.

This might seem like just stating the obvious or else like a sentimental greetings card stuff. Why do I know this for certain and think it's important? Why am I suddenly so definite?

It's because I have spent happy days reading the short stories in this book.

I read them slowly and thought about them for a long time. It is a fascinating look at Irish life and the way people are thinking in these our own times.

The entrants to the Powers Gold Label competition in aid of the Irish Hospice Foundation were asked to write around 450 words.

It's hard to give an impression of what matters in such a short space yet they do it very well, it's like opening up little windows into other people's minds and feelings. And through these windows they draw us into an amazing variety of scenes.

We come across the emigrant opening his parcel from home, the boy safe in a van eating chips after a match with his father, the old man combing his hair to go the funeral of his wife whom he still sees as his sweetheart after all these years, the pessimist who dreads the arrival of any letter beginning "Dear Sir" then gets a Dear Sir letter saying that his test results are benign.

This is a series of snapshots about what does matter to people. None of them are about financial gain, or personal recognition. These are not tales of triumphing over enemies, of making a killing, getting away with a gamble or pulling a fast one. They are about local heroes, poignant memories or images frozen in time.

What they have in common is that they are about loving and being loved.

This book reminds us, in a patchwork quilt of very different images, about what exercises our mind when someone asks us that cosmic question about what matters and what doesn't.

Suppose the spotlight was on you now, this minute and in a few paragraphs you had to tell us what something you would find worthy of celebrating, what would you choose?

You can't be vague and say something pious like the importance of living fully a good and caring life. Sorry for reverting to my school teaching days but that's not an answer to the question you are being asked.

You are asked to be specific and give us a glimpse of something an image that comes to mind quickly.

I think if I were doing it I would want to celebrate the wonderful shorthand of being part of a happy family where we can sit and re-live the past with humour and varying degrees of recall.

Or the company and laughter of friends over the years where we have known every emotion from triumph to disaster and back and can still find plenty to entertain us in the whole journey.

Or of falling in love in 1972 and hoping that it would all last for ever and ever and realising now that this was forty years and it has lasted so far!

Four thousand people in Ireland thought enough about this question to enter the competition and these little stories were all read by the judges who brought the number down to the fifty stories in this collection.

There will be some sense where you will recognise yourself, others which will fill you with sympathy and you will realise how lucky you are not to have had this loss or that pain. There will be others which open up worlds you knew nothing about.

The sponsors have arranged that the proceeds of this book go to the Irish Hospice Foundation.

For all of us who have known the unlimited care and help that the Hospice movement gives night and day for our loved ones this will be great news.

We need look no further to find and celebrate an example of what really matters.

Since writing this introduction Maeve Binchy died (on 30th July 2012), and our sympathies are with her husband Gordon Snell, their families and friends.

We would like to acknowledge and express our gratitude to Maeve and Gordon for their support of the Irish Hospice Foundation over the years.

Maeve Binchy, whose books are set in Ireland, won audiences all over the world. She was the international best-selling author of 15 novels and 10 collections of short stories. Throughout her career her name appeared at the top of bestsellers lists and lists of the most popular writers both at home and abroad. Considered a true Irish storyteller, Maeve remains without a doubt one of the most popular Irish novelists of the 21st Century.

She will be sadly missed.

Powers Whiskey, one of the great Irish symbols of quality, authenticity and tradition is delighted to showcase for the second year some of Ireland's hidden literary talent in 'Celebrating What Truly Matters: Powers Whiskey Short Story Collection, Volume II'.

This anthology was inspired by a hugely popular campaign for Powers which ran in the 1980s based on conversations and short stories. A nugget of social history, the campaign was an extraordinarily successful one, not only because of its wonderful, heart-warming stories and charming illustrations, but because everything sat so easily with the brand. It was a perfect fit, quintessentially Powers.

Penned by writers from across the country, this collection reflects on mellower moments in time and the warmth of relationships, family and friends. All proceeds will go towards supporting the Irish Hospice Foundation's range of programmes including the development of bereavement services, hospice services and development of palliative care in the community.

Why did we choose the theme 'Celebrating What Truly Matters'. Powers has always been woven into the heart of true Irish community. With a bottle pride of place in every Irish home, Powers has traditionally been the accompanying toast to mark all of life's occasion's - from the seemingly small to the highly significant. Building on this heritage and within the background of the great sociological changes that have swept the country we wanted to create an outlet for people to champion these moments of life through that quintessential Irish written form - the short story. By allowing people to share and create stories around this theme we hoped to create a forum for the Ireland and the Irish of today to express & celebrate what truly matters to them.

We would like to take this opportunity to thank each of the contributors for their creative efforts in 'Celebrating What Truly Matters', a selection box of stories that will live on in the inspirational work of the Irish Hospice Foundation.

ANNA MALMHAKE
CEO IRISH DISTILLERS PERNOD RICARD

Contents:

Courting

CONOR BOWMAN

*E*very time he drove past that church on his way to work there seemed to be a funeral taking place. He felt it was an omen; a mirroring of the slow death in his own heart. He'd grown tired and old and was still only forty-three. Philip Yeats, Senior Counsel and bachelor. He was footloose and mortgage-free.

"Any holiday plans?" his sister Rachel asked him by text, as he sat in the sweaty confines of Court 2 in the Round Hall. What she really meant was, "Found anyone to share your life with yet?" and, if he hadn't, then to feel free to join her and Richard and the three kids in Brittany in August. Again. He'd become weary of being tolerated by his own family, brought along to make up numbers. He wondered when he'd become this man, the one who got up early, came home late, watched his pension disappear on-line and dined alone.

Months ago he'd had a full MOT in the Blackrock Clinic. He'd half-hoped they might find something wrong. At least then his life would have been forced to change focus. Of course he'd been fine. He now wondered whether or not he'd really hoped for illness; the very act of giving Fate the fingers a distant aberration of memory. In the background, cases were being called and Yeats SC dozed as he waited to hear his client's name. But it was not his own case that awoke him.

"Number seventeen: 'In the Matter of the Succession Act and the Estate of Rosemary Veronica Cordial'," said the Probate Registrar.

His eyes snapped open as his soul was transported back more than two decades. He could smell the smoke of turf fires on the rain. He could feel the girl's hand in his. He doubted whether there could possibly be two people in the entire world with that same name. His heart beat faster. So, she never married, was his next thought.

"Your Honour," a voice said from the rear of the Court. The Judge beckoned the lay-litigant forward,

"Please take a seat at the front there. You are?"

"I'm Pippa Cordial, daughter of the…." she searched for the word she did not want and could not say.

"Rosemary Cordial was your mother, I take it?" said the Judge gently.

As he stood to allow the young lady into the bench beside him, the faintest of scents filled the Senior Counsel's being; turf fires near the Atlantic and the perfume her mother had always worn. He wondered what they would say to each other when they inevitably met. He would find the right words. Even the wrong ones would do for a start.

Beauty Salon

SUSAN O'CONNOR

S he thought about her last visit to a beauty salon. She had only gone in for a manicure and the girl, twenty at most, enthusiastically new, had been suggesting complementary treatments, upselling as they called it in the trade. Not that she didn't like to treat herself from time to time, she had just reached a stage of making the most of what God and the gene pool had given her. It was the hair today, the eight/ten weekly eradication of split ends and other signs of wear and tear. She always told the stylist she was going out later, they tried harder if they thought their work would be noticed. So she made up stories of reunions, family events and weekends away even if the reality was just general maintenance followed by a film and a bottle of wine at home.

It was important to like what you saw in the mirror, make all the excuses you want about weather, hormones, bad lighting and water retention – if you weren't reasonably content with what you had it was bad news, at least it had been for her. It had been no use hearing that she was always beautiful to him, she was talking nonsense and was imagining things. If she didn't like what she saw it ate away at her. Crash diets, spending a small fortune on "scientifically proven" creams and foundations, not to mention the miracle underwear. Dear Lord, what had she been thinking, when the uplifting/compressing underwear and the makeup came off she still hadn't liked what remained. So she got grumpy and stopped trying so hard, she hadn't become a slob, just wore comfy stuff and less make up. He still loved her but she wasn't happy in herself. Then she saw a programme about getting women to like themselves with no clothes on. She hadn't liked the presenter, a bit forward for her liking but spoke sense, no surgery or spending hours in the gym. Just learning to accept what you had and dress to suit. So she did it, got rid of anything she didn't want to grow into and anything she couldn't realistically ever shrink into. No more expensive lotions and potions and even if the hairdresser said it ruined her hair she kept swimming, she hated the gym with all its complicated machines but she liked swimming, she'd stick with that and just use conditioner.

So there she was, thirty something, finally copped on and focusing on what truly mattered, liking herself and believing it when other people did too. About time too, she thought, pushing open the salon door and deciding what story to tell the stylist today.

The Good Life

TADHG O'REGAN

When he opened the care package from mam he couldn't believe it Barry's tea, a few packets of Taytos, but best of all, his favourite drink, a one litre bottle of Powers Gold Label, best mother ever, it brought him close to tears. Sitting on the porch now he still couldn't bring himself to read the letter from Michelle that his mother had put in the package, she'll be finished her masters soon and heading off to Boston to start that internship, no internet out here, no mobile reception maybe he'll see if he can get a day off in town to Skype her before she goes, it'll be a long time before he gets to see her in person, she knows that too, a few more drinks and he'll have the courage to open that letter. A kangaroo jumps across the track a little way down and into some bushes. A few months ago that would have amazed him but now he was so used to seeing the damn things everywhere. Charlie rattles past in his battered old Toyota Hilux and gives a wave, probably off to shoot whatever poor endangered creature is feasting on his crops this evening. Sitting here in paradise surrounded by tropical plants and exotic creatures and all he can think about is home. A year ago if someone had told him he'd have full time work outside in the sunshine and fresh air every day, hunting wild pigs and fishing in crocodile infested billabongs in the evenings for fun he'd have probably collapsed and wept from excitement. God this Powers is good; it would be all the more tasty though in Rourke's with the boys watching the football. Man he'd love to be sitting in the pub now with the lads, or calling into Michelle to interrupt her studies, or even just sitting on the couch with mam and dad watching TV, the big fire going,

dad cracking jokes winding mam up. They had wanted him to go to college but he insisted on getting a trade, "electricians get good money" he'd said, "and people will always need electricity". That's what really mattered to a young man, good money, a full time job. Ha! And then Crash. Sure you can't live off the dole, miserable every day, arsing around at home or looking for a few nicksers, fifty quid here and there to put in an outside light for some aul wan. "No mon no fun". So off to Australia in search of what really mattered, and now as he sits here in paradise sipping on his favourite drink he realises what really matters and it's ten thousand miles away.

The Cross Word

HELENA NOLAN

"Incommunicado."

I looked up. For a second, I thought the man sitting opposite me was commenting on Kate but then I saw he had the newspaper folded, pen in hand and was looking across at his wife. She was knitting something purple, maybe a hat, but smiled up at him and asked "how many letters love?"

They had sat in beside us at the last station, right about the time Kate had stopped answering me. Now, she was staring out the window, as if only her stony frown was keeping the train in motion. Why were we always arguing? This latest row was about something as silly as whose fault it was that the coffee tasted sour.

"Proposal."

That was ironic. Kate and I seemed to have been arguing ever since her sister got engaged. It was like she was living someone else's future. I was getting sick of all the pre-wedding fuss and palaver. If I was honest, this latest row really started when I caught her looking at yet another bridal magazine in the station bookshop. I had stormed off in a huff, Kate following, upset, with the result that we had forgotten to buy our coffees and had no choice but the trolley on the rain.

"Living in the moment."

Was everything this man read out going to resonate with me today? If I was truly honest, what was holding me back was the past. I'd had my fingers burned before; I wasn't in any hurry to repeat the experience. But that wasn't Kate's fault. The woman took a tartan flask from her bag and carefully poured out two cups of steaming tea. He slipped a small bottle from his jacket, adding a splash of liquid gold to each cup. He caught me looking - "will you have a drop?"

"No thanks," I shook my head, embarrassed.

"Ah go on son," he said "it might make that stuff you have there a bit more drinkable."

I let him add a dash to both our cups. Kate was a polite girl. She nodded her thanks and took a sip and so did I. The man was right. Somehow the whiskey made the coffee taste sweeter, more mellow. I felt the knots in my stomach begin to loosen and was that the ice melting in Kate's eyes? A slow tear ran down her cheek. I loved her so much.

"Celebrating what truly matters."

"Powers," I said, smiling, finally identifying the warm, honeyed taste in my mouth. I held my hand out in an apology.

"No son, that doesn't fit."

"But it does," I thought, as Kate slipped her hand into mine; "it fits perfectly."

Puppy Love

SINEAD GILLETT

ew words had passed between the junior-seniors since the formulation of their plan, and even then few words had been spoken. Sitting side by side, laptop a piece, the elder had nudged his ally and turned his screen in invitation, careful to deter unsolicited eyes. The reaction was splendid. Agreement immediate. And a flurry of conversation fingered forth, their plan tapped out through muted Skype - no need for smiley faces. And now their plan was live. Slinking down the driveway they exchanged roguish glances. On the street eager steps set the pace. In less than a minute they were clear, celebrating the corner with no ordinary laughter. Long bass whoops the low beat to giddy, skidding shrieks of glee.

From a distance they resembled Charlie and Grandpa Joe en route to the chocolate factory – a skinny boy and a white-haired man with stick. Yet older and younger than that. It was the boy's brand-new, over-sized and grey uniform that slighted him. And the grandpa's cane held little purpose to his stride, a symbolic accessory of sorts. They were still to grow, and slow.

They were clearly junior-seniors.

On they marched, mirth-minded, through residential estates and then down older country roads. Sixty years between them, but equal junior-seniors, theirs was the kind of mischief that only came with such rank. Neither needed, nor were needed on. Their responsibility was coming of age. And that was the kind that required a pal.

The journey reached a gate, where a newish sign read 'Buyers to the Back'.

"Here we go," the elder boomed, lifting the latch with his stick.

"Should we go straight through?" the old boy asked, itching at the path.

The answer, "Straight to business," was quick, but not before that business was upon them.

The pup-dog whipped around in circles, junior-senior speed. The senior side of puppy, the junior side of dog, he was a small, lanky, scruffy thing clambering at their knees. Within minutes he was in their gang and he jigged on string beside them, tumbling, twisting and tugging along, home to face the music. On the way they passed a pub and the elder thought to stop. "He'll need some water don't you think? Sure we best get him a drop".

Sitting outside with pride they doted on the pup. Ignoring the water bowl, he gnawed the cane instead. It had been a masterful plan the owners agreed, clinking in celebration. The fizzy excitement of lemonade, the cosy comfort of Power's Whiskey, gulped and sipped in satisfaction. How best to toast the boy's first and the elder's last dog they'd share together?

Intention

FIONNUALA KENNY

"Lough Derg. I want to go to Lough Derg," she says.

"Why?"

"I have a special intention."

"Could you not say a decade of the rosary?"

Her eyes narrow.

"You told me to pick somewhere I wanted to go."

I was thinking of lunch in town or a picture, maybe. Fat chance.

"So you want to commune with a higher power?"

"A few prayers wouldn't do you any harm!"

"You can hardly walk!" I protest. A lifetime of forcing the feet into high heels. Now they're like monkey nuts, curled and gnarled and knobbly.

"They do day tours now" she sniffs.

It's worse than I imagined. The rain sheeting across us, the winds stinging hands and face. The priest intoning and the people's sighing responses. The dirge-like praying, as if waiting for death. I draw her arm through mine, hold her hand. I feel the bones nestled in the papery skin, as if I held a tiny bird.

"I forgot me gloves" she says.

I take mine off. Protesting, she lets me put them on her. She's like a scarecrow, tiny, with huge flapping hands.

"You were always very big," she says. "I don't know where you came from."

She looks out across the lake. The water is lapping the shore, mutinous and sullen. It rasps along the pebbles.

"I remember the first time you walked," she says. "Portrane. Your Father stood you up. Ten months, that's all you were. I thought you'd fall, but he knew. Next minute, you'd staggered over to me!"

She laughs.

"You've been running ever since" she says.

I can hardly lift my head in the driving rain. She's soaked.

"You think you'll be a terrible Mother" she says. "But you don't know. A child can change all that. You were such a good child. I don't know what I'd have done, only for you."

We're waiting for the boat to go back. She's shivering. Her lips are blue.

"Now that you've communed with the higher powers, will you commune with the Powers that be?" I ask, taking a bottle from my bag. A baby, they always called it. A baby Powers.

"Is that Holy Water?" she asks.

"In a manner of speaking," I say.

The gloves are clumsy. She takes them off, takes a warming, welcome sip.

"Will you tell me your intention?" I ask.

"That you learn what really matters before it's too late," she says. "Of course, I prayed for smaller feet for it. You have terrible big feet. That's why you were able to walk so young."

Plus One

CAROLINE McCALL

"kype?"

"Yes, Nana."

"On the computer?"

"Yes, Nana. I'll have it set up in a minute."

"And I'll be able to see Laura? At the wedding in New York?"

Brendan sighed. "Yes, Nana and they'll be able to see you too."

Maisie brushed the crumbs from her blue cardigan. "You should have told me sooner. I'll never make it back up the stairs to get changed."

"You're fine, Nana. Honestly."

"Are you sure, Brendan? Maybe I should wear the pink one?"

"The blue one's fine, Nana." Brendan adjusted the camera until her image appeared on the screen.

Maisie looked at the wrinkled face staring back at her. "I suppose I'm not bad for ninety two."

"Ninety one, Nana. You're not ninety two 'til September. Now, are you ready?

"Ah, go on then." Maisie sipped her tea. "It's getting cold, Michael."

"I'm Brendan, Nana."

"Of course you're Brendan. That's what I said."

"Will I warm it up for you?"

He went to the glass cabinet. Among the tea cups, the all Ireland medals and the souvenirs from around the world, was a bottle of Powers.

"Just a drop then." She watched him pour the golden liquid into her tea. "That's plenty. Am I on yet?"

"Soon, Nana."

"Your granddad loved a drop of Powers." Maisie took a sip from her mug. "Thirty seven years dead, Lord rest him. He never saw her you know."

"Who, Nana?"

"Laura. And now she's getting married to that Yank."

"It's Hank, Nana."

"Hank, Yank, it's all the one. He's a fine looking fella all the same. Just like your granddad."

Maisie took another sip from her mug. "That's a grand drop."

The computer screen buzzed to life revealing a large ballroom, with guests sitting around tables chatting. "I can see them, Brendan. Can they see me?"

"Soon, Nana."

"There she is."

A pale face filled the screen. "Nana, it's Laura. Can you hear me?"

"Hi, Mrs O'Callaghan. Hi, Brendan, it's Hank. We're delighted that you could be here."

"You look beautiful, Laura." Maisie dabbed her eyes with a tissue. "Did you get the few bob I sent you?"

Laura smiled. "Yes, Nana. We're going to buy a dinner service with it and we'll think of you every time we use it. And we'll be home in September for your birthday. Nana I ...."

The screen went blank. Brendan tapped the keyboard but nothing happened.

Maisie took another sip of tea. "That'll be your 3G card, Brendan. It wouldn't have happened if you'd used my broadband."

"You have a computer, Nana?"

Of course I have, Brendan." Maisie opened a drawer to reveal a sleek, black laptop.

"But I couldn't go to a wedding on my own."

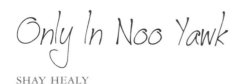

Only In Noo Yawk

SHAY HEALY

As the black limousine crested the hill to reveal the first glimpse of the New York skyline, the driver hit a button on his dashboard and out came Frank Sinatra.

" Start spreading the noos…"

"You've a brass neck," I laughed.

"Yer foist time?"

"Yeah."

"I can tell….never get it wrong"

What are the signs?"

"Edgy.. afraid of me an' my black limo."

The banter continued all the way to my hotel on 53rd Street. I took the bottle of Powers from its box and slipped it deep into my overcoat pocket. If I got the job it would be a celebratory gift.

Out on the street again, I raised my arm to hail an approaching taxi. Twenty yards to my right, a fur-coated woman was flapping her arms like a swan trying to take off from the canal at Portobello Harbour.

To my surprise, the cab passed her by and pulled in alongside me. The driver looked and sounded like Joe Pesci.

"D'ya know why I pulled in for you instead of dat broad wavin' her arms around?

"Tell me."

"Broads like dat are so busy wavin'…they don't have time to give you no tip."

I hear you" I said. "No fuss.

"Ya got it…so what are you doin' in Noo Yawk"

"I'm Irish…. here for a job interview with a PR company."

When we pulled up to the office skyscraper on 5th Avenue, I tipped him three dollars.

"Good luck…and remember….no fuss."

The interview went brilliantly well and I got the job. I pulled the bottle of Powers from my coat pocket.

"I brought this for you. "

"Irish whiskey." My new boss crossed to a cabinet and took out two whiskeys glasses.

"Slainte," I said.

"Salut," he responded. "That's smooth whiskey….now let's go grab a bite of lunch."

Fifth Avenue was teeming with people and traffic. My new boss started waving his arms over his head to attract a taxi. He wasn't having much luck and I dared myself to interrupt him.

"I know I've only been in New York for a couple of hours, but would you mind if I try?" He looked at me quizzically.

"Be my guest."

I raised my arm to shoulder height and extended my forefinger upwards. In the space of ten seconds, a taxi pulled in beside us. I could see my new boss was amused as well as intrigued, but he said nothing, opened the door and followed me into the back seat.

The taxi slid back out into the traffic, but before my new boss even had time to state our destination, the driver swivelled his head and gave me his Joe Pesci smile.

"Well Irish…didja get the job?"

Lines Written On A Seat

JOESPH FRAYNE

She was sitting beside Patrick Kavanagh on his seat, he gazing at the water through his greeny specs. She looked gorgeous. It would have been a bit obvious to go straight over to her, though that's what I wanted to do but there wasn't much room with immovable Paddy there. So I hovered at the other side of the canal reading 'O commemorate me where there is water' and glancing across every few seconds to see if she'd notice me. I'd seen her there before, so I had a plan.

When my old English teacher brought us on a pilgrimage to honour the poet, this was a spot we'd come to. How grown up we felt when he'd shown us all the pubs the poet loved! I didn't think the poems we'd learned had really sunk in but I found myself remembering some of them.

I crossed the footbridge to approach her, determined it would be no banal introduction.

"How are you?" I said.

"Fine," she said.

"What's your name?" I blundered on.

"Olga," she said.

I managed to say a few lines of the water poem and she smiled a big broad smile and we got chatting after that and then I suggested - if she was interested - that I'd show her a few of the poet's favourite places, that we could explore

them together. I pointed out where Parsons bookshop used to be and we walked to The Waterloo and Searson's and Raglan Road.

I could tell she was impressed.

That night we met in a pub off Grafton Street,

"This used to be a church," I said.

She didn't believe me and said that I'd the gift of the gab and it sounded funny the way she said it with her accent.

The pair of us got on so well that we began to see a lot of each other, sharing things we liked about each other's countries and one time we shared a meal on a barge that came all the way from Athy. Now we share everything.

The day we were married was a soft Irish day, the sun turning out silver linings in every cloud and Olga's mother crying with joy - everything just as it should be.

We have two children now, Nicolae (mad into hurling) and Geta (loves art). It's been a journey that I wouldn't have missed. The other day Olga told me she'd done a thesis on the Irish poets for her doctorate before she came to Ireland.

"So you knew all about Kavanagh when we met?" I said.

"Yes," she said, "of course."

Verbose

HUGH HYNES

"What does 'verbose' mean, Denis?" asked Flaherty as he gave up on the crossword.

"Verbose? Spell it," shouted the barman from the back room.

"V-E-R-B-O-S-E."

The barman paused for a moment, "Verbose….no, not a clue."

Flaherty stared at the fire in the empty pub for another few minutes ruminating over his next topic starter, one more successful than the last hopefully. He aimed his voice once more towards the bar. "Have you ever heard the Corncrake?"

"Oh I've often heard the guttural 'crex-crex' of that ground-loving bird as it called to its mate across the windswept banks of the Shannon Callows, why do you ask?"

"Just wondering really, I haven't heard one in years," said Flaherty, raising his glass slightly to silently indicate his need for another drink.

"I hear they're endangered" said Flaherty breaking a few minutes of silence.

"The Verboses?"

"Ah no, the Corncrake."

"The Verboses are ok so?"

"I don't get you."

"You said the Verbose wasn't endangered."

"Yes it's the Corncrake that's in trouble."

"Right, you can shoot the Verbose then?"

"I suppose so, it's a bird is it? I thought you didn't know what it was?"

"You said it was a bird."

"The endangered corncrake I meant."

"Ah I have you."

The barman went around back once more. Flaherty picked up his crossword again, disappointed that their avian discussion had ended in confusion. "Obtuse" was another word he didn't know but he decided not to bother Denis with it.

"Do you know what 'non sequitur' means, Denis?" he eventually asked when the barman reappeared again.

"He was a good handicapper for Ken Oliver....won the Massey Ferguson Gold Cup in a common canter, hell of a horse," recounted the barman. Flaherty was no wiser as to the meaning of the Latin phrase and thought he hadn't been heard correctly but he listened to the barman's racing reminiscences with interest nonetheless.

It was getting late and Flaherty liked to be home before midnight so he called one more for the road and drank up, the crossword was only half done and he'd gone wrong on the Sudoku but at least he'd got himself out of the house and he enjoyed having his whisky by the fire.

"Good luck then, Denis."

"Richard Pitman, if memory serves," said the barman.

Confused, Flaherty walked away home with more questions than answers but he valued the bit of company of an evening, especially since Lily died, and that's what truly mattered.

The Nest

BRENDAN FRAWLEY

S usan spots it first. A perfect little nest with 5 eggs inside. She's the eldest and taller so that makes it easier. Of course, I'm not wearing my glasses either. Mam will kill me if she finds out but the eye doctor said I have to wear a patch on one side to strengthen my bad eye. As if the glasses weren't ugly enough.

The eggs are gorgeous - pale blue with rusty coloured spots. Sue says we mustn't tell anyone because if the Barrys find out they will surely smash them just for fun. And then the little baby chicks will never be born. Those Barrys are such bold boys, always fighting and shouting and calling me 'fatty four-eyes'. I hate them.

All weekend we sneak out to the green to visit the nest and make sure it is safe. Dad's book says there might be baby chicks in a week or maybe two. 'We can give them names,' I say.

Sue rolls her eyes and says I am thick. She warns me not to tell anyone in school on Monday. The Barrys will find out if I do. 'I know that,' I say. 'Just because you have your First Communion made doesn't mean you know everything.'

I can think of nothing else as we walk to school on Monday morning. Miss O'Donoghue begins class with 'Our Father' and then it is news time. Who has news today? Noelle is telling us about her new baby brother again. My news is much better than Gerard Carmody started crawling. I want to tell but Sue will go mad and never play with me again. She only played with me last weekend because her friend was at her mobile home in Kilkee.

I take a chance. I raise my hand and tell everyone about the nest, the eggs, the baby chicks. Everyone is looking at me, listening to me. It is brilliant. Noelle is raging. Only then do I remember that Noelle Carmody is Tommy Barry's cousin.

All day I have a big knot in my tummy. On the walk home I tell Susan what I did. She goes white and starts to run. I chase after as fast as I can. We reach the green and see the Barrys running towards us. As they pass, Tommy hits me a dig and I fall. They all laugh and keep going. We run to where the nest lies broken on the ground, five smashed eggs beside it. My eyes smart and I start to cry. Susan looks at me. I expect to see anger, not tears in her eyes. She gives me a hug. We turn and together head home for tea.

A Boat to the Blaskets

MÁIRÍN O'SHEA

A fine rain swings in the mist as we set off, her looking like a slender quivering feather, in a life jacket that would have wrapped around her thrice. The boat slices the incoming waves as it pulls out, and she grips the steel bar so that the paper-thin layer of skin between her bones and the salty spray stretches taut.

It would have been easy not to have come down this week. To have continued losing touch with the people and places that are map markings for home, spending all these windy Wednesdays forgetting myself in pursuit of someone else's dubious ends. I could have kept going, kept watching myself keep going, while all sense of congruence between origin and destination slowly ebbed out of my life and down into the silent drain of disillusionment.

Defecting the money machine and jumping overboard is difficult, but learning the hard way means learning well that in finding yourself totally at sea, an internal compass resurfaces. One that allows even this cailín caillte to cast any lingering doubts into the whipping Atlantic wind. I am searching for shore now because I know another day a different wind will come, the quiet whispering breeze that tells you the boat is sinking and the time is gone.

And I think of that breeze as I watch her face, think about how the soft breath of that final wind will one day pull on the embers of what glows here now. One day, none of the rest will matter, because we will be separated by a wooden box and one heart still beating; a black car will pull out from a church on a hill and I will walk behind her, or she will walk behind me. One day one of us will go back to being dust, and then, no time to wonder from where the gift of these days came or where it is that they go.

So here I find myself, holding fast to a rail on a slippery deck and my heart soaring with the joy of being beside her, watching her sway on her spindly legs and laugh with real, grateful-to-God happiness as a wish is granted. To be near her is to know what is right in the world when the darkness of all that is wrong starts to close in. This is the life-raft of what truly matters and for her I throw my thanks to the sea and celebrate this day in my soul, seeing hers dancing on the waves. My name giver, my fire lighter, my stoic hero. My grandmother – smiling on a boat to the Blaskets.

Heels

DECLAN McCORMACK

*L*ouise Barber had long legs which, her pupils noticed, began in her shiny black clacketty shoes. Some days she wore high heels and some days ('the small days' as her pupils disapprovingly dubbed them) low heels.

The girls liked her tall days. Everything seemed more real and solid and noisy when Miss Barber wore high heels. She seemed more animated, and the school-day passed quicker in 3G.

It was during one such high heel noisy day that Miss Barber shocked them all by suddenly crumpling up (that's what it looked like to class) and then slumped down (that's what it looked like) in her teacher's chair where she usually only sat when they were having a 'teigh a chodhladh'.

Best friends Sophie Nugent and Christina Creamer exchanged bewildered expressions. Sophie wondered if it was because of the mad weather. It had been like Summer for a week and then it was like Winter with the sea all stormed up (as her mum described it). White waves in the bay, cherry blossoms blown everywhere, tulips losing their petals. Which was sad. Very fat petals, Sophie noticed.

After what seemed like AGES to her pupils, Miss Barber mumbled something (normally Miss Barber NEVER EVER mumbled) about she or someone else thinking they were going to die. Sophie wondered if Miss had nearly been murdered which often happens in the television late at night when mum is watching TV by herself and dad is on the computer.

Miss said that one thing she had learned from Cassie (Cassie who?) was to enjoy the simple pleasures, to realise how beautiful everything was. Things like grass, sky, mountains, people, toast. She asked them when they went home to write down the things they loved. "Anything could be on the list," she said. "Loop the Loop lollies, Love Heart sweets," (she was crying again) "Mikado biscuits, anything. Your friends. Your gran's scones."

Miranda Parsons said she HATED scones and her gran had very thin hands that frightened her. Miss laughed which only made her wet eyes sparkle even more. She was dabbing her eyes and nose in a little hanky. Pity she hadn't got a towel, Sophie thought.

Next day Miss took up all the lists and the day after she said she found the lists wonderful but would not 'disclose' them as some people might be embarrassed.

Sophie and Christina thought this was stupid. Why would anyone be embarrassed over what you love.

They noticed one thing though which WAS very strange. Miss Barber never wore low heels after that day. Maybe that's what embarrassed meant. Finding out everyone hated your low heels.

Tinkering with the Massey

FIONA STEVENSON

*I*t is an unsettling thing to witness a person's life condensed into five sheets of paper, within a blue folder, and see it stacked amongst others on a trolley at the end of the ward. I could, right now, salvage it from the pile and keep it. I want to do this because it will be the only proof that we were here. The cover tells his name, that his birth was in 1930, where we live, and that I am his wife and next of kin. Recorded on the inner pages are medications given and clinical observations. All facts to confirm this is a man who is alive, still viable.

I know I will need this evidence to comfort me when I am finally alone. What I do not quite understand though, is the desperate urgency to possess it that consumes me suddenly. More lucidly, I realise his medical notes are essential to him now, and of no consolation to me yet, so I leave them untouched.

The curtains remain half closed. I smooth the bed covers and the back of his hand. There was a time rubbing his hand would have made him flinch, and after a time irritated him, as he is a man not given to emotion or sentimentality. Yet, he had always been constant and solid, both in stature and character. He stirred slightly then, exhaling a raw, pitiful groan.

"Joe, are you all right? Do you want me to wet your lips for you?" I wipe a small wet sponge across his parched mouth.

An invisible line has been drawn down the centre of his body. The right side, which is nearest me, is familiar and warm. The complete left side has just completely fallen away from the midline, bloodless and drooped. He is half dead.

The nurse explains about strokes and how it would be a long road to partial rehabilitation. Joe and I listen and I nod for both of us. She leaves me holding a booklet. Joe tries turning his head to look at me in total protest, but his neck will not move. He begins to leak tears of loss and frustration that mix with mine as I hold his face.

"Close your eyes Joe. Have a rest for a minute."

Joe chases the collie through the barley field and tinkers on Easter morning with the Massey in the barn. He shares a joke and a hot Powers with the vet after delivering the calf on a bitter November night. He spreads far too much butter on the soda bread, and knowing I've caught him smiles and winks. I make us a pot of strong tea and sit beside him.

Trust

SINEAD COTTER

"Now, Kevin," the solicitor said. "Do you understand what Enduring Power of Attorney is?"

My father hesitated. I looked down at my hands, then around at the office's bare walls. It was cold. I shivered.

"It's when someone can't manage his own affairs, and the family takes over."

The solicitor knew my father, but it had been years since they'd met. He had to make sure Dad was still of sound mind.

"That's right. Let me just take you through it."

My Dad was eighty-five, and a few weeks previously he'd asked me whether I remembered something that had happened at his wedding. "No, Dad," I said. "I wasn't born." It was the look on his face when he realised what he'd said that killed me.

"So if you lost your mental capacity, this document would give Karen control of your affairs. I need to be sure you understand that, so can you tell me again, please, what you think it involves?"

My father was sitting upright, alert. This wasn't easy for him.

"I know she'd be able to sell the house out from under me." We used to joke about this, but it didn't seem so funny now.

"Yes. So you'd have to be able to trust her."

That was a hard one. My Dad wasn't a man for compliments or praise; he might feel something but he wouldn't say it. Now he tried to make a joke of it.

"She hasn't given me much choice!"

In the outer office I helped him do up his coat. "Honestly, Dad," I scolded gently. "Would it have killed you to say something nice about me?"

"Sure he knew I didn't mean it."

A bitter wind blew us down the street past a pub. I stopped. "Come on. We need something after that."

Inside, Dad gave me money and I went to the bar. A hot whiskey for him, tea for me. I stuffed the change in my pocket and brought over the drinks.

"Sláinte." I took a sip of his whiskey, warm and mellow, and began to feel better. "Still, that went okay."

"It had to be done," he agreed sadly. I touched his hand. "It's like insurance, Dad. We'll never need it."

He nodded and picked up his drink. "Speaking of forgetting things, where's my change?"

"Sorry." I gave him the money and he put it away without looking at it.

"So," I said archly. "Aren't you going to check it?"

"Not at all." He tipped his glass at me, his face shining suddenly with a young man's glee, that matched the pleasure in my own face when he said then, simply, "Sure don't I trust you?"

Shuffle & Deal

JOE KEARNEY

M any would call it a children's game, but it's our game, it's our choreography. She hasn't spoken in over five years, although lately I hear her voice.

You see, I was never a great listener, always off somewhere inside my head and, then there was the music. Always my grand passion, music. It's hard to be a listener when you're plugged in; first there were the stereo headphones, with the trailing kink of cable, then the Walkman and the Discman. She never shared my taste for heavy rock, so I took to listening alone.

Oh, she was a high flyer once, in the days of power dressing, all shoulder-pads, high heels and wide hair - advertising, she was big in advertising. I know you'll laugh when you see her now, but she wasn't always like this. Me. I was a scruff-bucket. Loved the counter job in the store, a builder's suppliers. I haven't changed much except the hair is thinner and grey and, of course that extra stone or so. I still have the ponytail and the boot-cut jeans and I try to wear my Birks as often as the weather allows. I'm an iPod man now though, 10,000 songs.

So here we are most evenings. I move the food tray in front of her, fluff up the pillows and start to deal. She comes to life with the first slap of the cards. Often a nurse will come in to watch. They are amazed how someone with no interest in the world can come to life over a card game, but there it is—Switch. Five cards each, we use the complex version, seven skips, the Jack reverses, play a two with a two and no Jokers—three lives apiece. Sometimes she smiles when she takes that last life from me…and it always does.

I've sold the house; had to, this place is expensive and they retired me early. I found the box of cassettes during the move. The label says ex-TV 1972. That was when I heard her voice again. I remembered making them holding a microphone in front of the TV, The Old Grey Whistle Test. She must have come into the room while I had the headphones on.

"Frankie." she says. She only called me Frankie at special times. "Frankie, I've got to talk to you. I need your help. Frankie please, it's important!"

The words are clear above All The Young Dudes. Then the door slams. I've listened back to all the tapes, even the white-noise hiss, but that's all I can find of her voice.

I was always a bad listener, but now we have the cards, so we shuffle and deal. That's all that matters.

This

FRANK McCAUGHEY

*T*ea from a china cup does taste different. Smoother. Two beautiful chocolate coated shortbread biscuits grace the saucer. I reluctantly bite into one. Anticipation can be enough. A tsunami of tea gushes into my mouth melting the chocolate and splitting the biscuit apart. My teeth and tongue jump in for the kill.

Governor O'Sullivan is staring at me. Not sure for how long. Time has long since dissolved away. It is a concept. Time is simply the mind trying to give structure to one moment appearing after another in infinity. This is infinity. This is the big bang. And it is always missed. Sensations in the mouth. Hand moving. Thoughts appearing. Sounds appearing.

"We cannot give you back these years Tom..." The governor shakes his head from left to right. Thinking about the first time this office appeared. Thinking happens by itself. Try and create a thought if you don't believe me. Breathing happens by itself. This now is eternity renewing itself with every breath.

"A lot of men don't survive what you have been through Tom. And on the outside, life is more chaotic than ever. People have no time for anything. You will need to make use of all the services available to you....." Outside and inside. There is no inner and outer. There is only what appears.

"You think they are all free out there. Well they're not. They live their lives in tower blocks high up above life. With that money Tom you have a chance to live more than people might do in their whole life. You will have time and money to really figure out what matters and pursue it."

The cup is placed back down on the saucer. A black bird perches on the ledge outside the window. It looks through the bars. It does not try to be happy. It simply is. Why is happy better than sad. Happy is happy. And sad is sad. Prison has taught me, there is no prison. Everything just is. Despite all the thoughts appearing to the contrary, there is nothing bad or good.

"Do you have anybody coming to collect you Tom?" The thought appears about Susan. "My lawyer has said she will be here" the words appear in reply. A biscuit appears inside the mouth again. The symphony of tea and tongue and teeth and chocolate and crunching. It is everything. I have no concept of meaning. Life has no meaning. It is its own meaning. Nothing matters. And when that is seen, then everything matters. Life as it is, is enough. A cup of tea is now all that matters. This now is all there is.

Everything else is a story.

Morning

ALISON McKEOWN

Mr Delaney checked for scuff marks and lint, and satisfied, closed the door behind him, making his way out into the day. Ah Mrs Sweeney, isn't it glorious? (Tip the hat). Spring has sprung, indeed. Into the Post Office for the pension, two stamps please, Paddy. Shocking about that shower above in Leinster House! Sure they have us in this mess. Then into Smiths for a loaf and the paper, Health Supplement today. Betty used to love it. Always telling me what new disease I had today... Ah there's himself! And look at that grand little bowler with ye, that's a proper doggy. Look what I have for Buster today! Reaching into the paper bag, he pulls out a morsel of its treasures for the little waggy tail. Pleasantries exchanged, it's over for the 10 o'clock Mass. The kneeling is a killer, offer it up.

He always thinks of her here. She'd mutter under her breath about Mrs So-and-so whose husband was a demon for the drink; and "Would you look at that O'Dea wan, is she off to a dance at the Gresham or to a Funeral?" He smiles. She could be an awful woman. He looks up at the stained glass. The workmanship in that! Isn't that something? Betty never missed the 10 o'clock. He'd never had much truck with it himself. Went along with it because it was what you did, until the girls got older and that ended that. Betty would complain, but sure look how that lot turned out!

The fella saying the Mass today was an African chappie. Father Gabriel. From Sudan. Would you credit it?! That was the way of the world now. And in fairness, he was an awful decent lad. When he first started visiting him after Betty went, he wasn't too happy. He wouldn't be calling him "Father". And he couldn't talk about her. But then, one Thursday, he brought a bottle, starting the weekly ritual of a good chess game and a nice glass of Powers, putting the world to rights. He couldn't be like that with the girls. They'd been closer to their Mam. They had their own lives.

Mr. Delaney only started the 10 o'clock when Betty, too ill to walk, asked him to go in her place. After she was gone, he carried on. It was a good way to fill the hour. He didn't really listen, but he felt close to her here. And afterwards, the best part of the day. Into the park and over to the pond. Here ye go lads – out with the rich pickings, warm brown crumbs, the little ducks fighting their way into the fray to get their daily bread.

Harry Ordinary

CONOR WILLIAMS

*D*uring a recent international rugby match between France and England, a seasoned Irish commentator noted how it took him some time to be able to correctly pronounce the surname of the French number eight, Imanol Harinordoquy. When he made his debut in 2002, many of those in the sports journalism community simply referred to him as 'Harry Ordinary'.

Hearing this sobriquet put me in mind of a chance encounter I had with a true Irish legend more than twenty years ago. In the summer of 1989, I met former professional golfer, the late Harry Bradshaw, during the second round of the Irish Open Championship at Portmarnock. Harry was the Rory McIlroy of his day, part of Ireland's World Cup winning team in 1958 and famously losing a playoff for the British Open Championship to Bobby Locke in 1949, having elected to play his second shot at the fifth hole as it lay, from a broken bottle.

Harry remarked to me how he found it difficult to accept the exorbitant purses paid to modern professional athletes, particularly in his own sport. I cannot recall his exact words but to paraphrase, it went something like this: no matter how much money you have, you can live in one house at a time; drive one car at a time; eat one meal at a time. Modern sports professionals, he said, rarely see this; the culture of instant sensual gratification has tricked them into believing it is possible to have it all and to have it now.

Harry was wearing a green blazer, similar to the one donned by the winner of the U.S. Masters golf tournament, although he never had the fortune to win a Major. We sat at the back of the seventeenth green together for a few moments longer, watching Australian Graham Marsh hole out for a par four before Harry folded up his seat and moved on to watch the action on the final hole.

Harry's words have stayed with me. Priorities change as we grow older, what we think is critical at ten years old becomes trivia at forty. However, living modestly in the moment is the debt we owe to those who go before us because we cannot be sure of tomorrow's task.

The Garden

MIRIAM O'MEARA

*T*he first time I met her, she had just sprayed me with a hose. Laughter exploded before her gardening hat appeared above hydrangea bushes. Then I saw her face.

"I'm sorry."

"That's okay." I replied, though my dress was soaking.

"I've drenched you. Come in for a cup of coffee and a towel to dry off."

I wasn't sure whether the deluge was entirely accidental, or designed to initiate a conversation. Either way, it was the start of our friendship.

She smelt like her garden that was full of exotic plants growing impossibly where they shouldn't have been able to.

"What's your secret?"

"I invite everything into the garden, those that want to stay, survive."

"They do more than that." I said, staring at the riot of colour which bloomed that summer; their perfumes intoxicating the air.

Our birthdays were on the same day in spring.

"Next birthday, we will have champagne in that hotel where we can't possibly afford to have more than one glass. We'll sip slowly and people watch in a world where we wouldn't want to live anyway, but wish to spend an afternoon in. We can put on our flimsiest glad rags and look like we belong."

It didn't happen like that though. Not quite.

"Look at my garden. I just don't have the energy anymore."

"I could help you, though I don't have your green fingers."

The brasher plants had started to suffocate the tender ones as if the cruelty of nature now controlled the garden not her.

"Remember our birthday promise to ourselves."

"I can't go out."

She pulled the wig off, revealing her baldness. I couldn't think of anything to say.

"What about a Gatsby look?"

I pulled off the long silken scarf that was tied around my waist and threw it to her. She wrapped it around her head, tying it into a bow at the side.

"You see. Everyone will think it's the latest style and copy us."

So we went to the hotel though she pushed her glass of champagne aside.

"I've lost my taste for that. You take mine. At these prices we can't afford to waste it."

Then she laughed that wonderful infectious chortle.

So she drank Chinese tea where the flower buds unravelled like ribbons of purple in the glass teapot.

"This is the best birthday I've ever had."

I wanted to cry. Maybe she knew that, so she pointed out to the hotel garden renowned for its horticulture.

"I would have liked to have had a garden as big as that one."

"But yours is more beautiful."

And it was.

Memories of Gold

HUGH FULHAM-McQUILLAN

"We've made it, sonny Jim. Another week, and I'm still standing." Every Sunday evening, my grandad said these words as he eased himself up out of his armchair and across to the drinks cabinet. Throwing open the doors, he'd ask, "What will it be, mister?"

"Whatever you're having yourself, Jack," I'd say. He'd chuckle and pretend not to hear, and I'd always wonder if this was part of the act, I'd say it louder. He'd pour orange juice into a heavy glass which, in my small hands, felt like it had been carved from the solid floor of a crystal cave.

After pouring himself a dram of Power's Gold label, he'd run his finger across the spines on the shelf, pause, select a book, and fold himself back into his armchair. I'd swish the orange juice in my cavernous glass and wonder what it would be like to be grown up and have such big hands. Gradually, his voice would quieten my thoughts, bringing me on a journey between the lines and through the pages, until sleep found me nestled between the covers.

On the day I lost my job, sitting in the kitchen, I said to my fiancé, "At least we're still standing."

On the day I almost got married, I drove to his house and he sat me down. It took him a little longer to reach the cabinet. "What will it be, mister?"

"What ever you're having yourself, Jack." He poured a dram of amber into each glass. The conversation soon turned to books, and I read him this short story. With a grave face, he said, "You're missing an ending." He then told me about people I'd never met and I wasn't sure if he had either, but I was content and closed my eyes as the stories tumbled through the air like bumble bees in August.

On the day of his funeral, I rearranged his long life of words into a eulogy about a man who introduced me to many fine things, who taught me to appreciate life and all its rough edges, to celebrate the rising of the sun each day like it was a newborn. I thought I had my ending. But I grew older, and older, still. And now I have my own little man, who every Sunday evening, I ask "What will it be, mister?" He replies in his most serious voice, "Whatever you're having yourself, Jim." We toast granddad Jack and I read aloud, book in one hand, Gold label in the other, as he sleepily peers over the tumbler of orange juice clasped in his hands.

This story will never end.

You Own the View

WINTER HYNES

It was always my ambition to live in a small white cottage by the sea in Connemara. My father used to bring me out to Lettermullen as a boy to visit an old friend of his, a retired judge. Watching the surrounding hills disappear and reappear mystified me. Soft rain coming in from the Atlantic washed my face, cleansed my soul and changed me forever.

For twenty five years I laboured at various enterprises in an attempt to save enough money to buy my earthly paradise. I was never successful but I never went hungry. I told myself that the early mornings and long commutes were a sacrifice worth making. That tomorrow would bring the rewards for today's labour. I was arrogant enough to believe I could climb Mount Purgatory on a Woodies' ladder.

My father used to ask me why I was working so hard. "What is it you are working for?" he would ask.

"I work for the same reason everyone does," I'd say. "To achieve something. To be someone."

"But you are someone," he'd say.

"I know, but I want my cottage in Connemara and I'm not going to get it any other way."

"Well be careful you don't lose today in tomorrow's dreams."

It wasn't the recession or global instability that brought me down. The weight of the truth was simply too much to carry any longer. The ladder broke. I slipped and fell. Down through twenty five years of lost opportunities, broken promises and wasted moments. Falling, my life flashed before me. Something my father had said not long before he died echoed from the cliffs in my mind. "Nightmares begin when dreams end. You only live once no matter what we pretend."

I lost everything including my wife, my business and my home. I was broke in every sense of the word. I indulged myself in self pity, lingering as the late repentant for quite some time.

It was a winter's day when the sun broke through. Out of the blue I remembered something I had long forgotten. I got up from the bench in the Iveagh Gardens and walked for seven days to the Spanish Arch. Along the way I purged myself, shedding the last of my deadly possessions, one for each day.

I awoke this morning in my little white cottage which I rent from the Sisters of Mercy. Handing over the keys, Sister Catherine said to me "You can rent the house but you own the view." I went for a walk on Dog's Bay Beach. Soft rain came in from the Atlantic, washed my face and cleansed my soul. Tonight I'll gaze at the stars.

Apres-Match

CHRISTINA GALVIN

*I*t was the heady whiff of them that would get you. They could only be eaten hot, at midnight after the county final, inside a red 1981 Datsun Sunny with rusting bumper, parked with the engine running and the heater on full-blast on a half-lit backstreet somewhere in the outskirts of Cork, and you both looking out the windscreen at the rain pinging the puddles, wipers going swish, swish, thwack, swish, swish, thwack…

And you would tear open the paper packs of salt and smother the chips before biting the corners off wee pouches of vinegar for the second necessary round of liberal pickling. Then you'd take one between thumb and forefinger, just one thick, limp chip and blow real slow. And the smell would make you all woozy, rushing blood through limbs to lips and you'd bare your teeth for the chomp like a horse preparing to whinny and end up burning your bloody tongue anyway but it wouldn't really matter 'cos your tastebuds would be lepping and your belly would swelling with a barrelful of giddiness. And you could feel your cheeks go all pink and you'd sit there in the front seat beside your father, neither of you needing to speak, with a parcel each of the greasiest, chunkiest chips wrapped in newspaper and them warming your laps and filling the air with snugness. It didn't matter that your team had been trounced 'cos there you were, the two of you, and you both staring straight ahead with your heads pure empty, munching away and slurping coke from ice-cold cans and the hungry breath from your nostrils mingling with steam from the chips and windows misting. And it was deadly, it was

- like this instant had somehow spilt outside of time and this was the only place in the whole world you and your da were meant to be right then.

"Right then," your da would say, licking his lips and wiping his mouth on the grubby sleeve of his anorak. "You ready, Jack?" And he'd look at you and smile one of his big, generous smiles. Then he'd passed his scraps to you and you'd bundle up the newspaper in one big ball, mash the empty cans with the heel of your boot and bung the rubbish in the back seat. The car would putter off then, rain hacking the roof. Creaking the seat back as far as it would go, you'd squeeze your knees to your chest, rub the mist from the window and gaze out at the night-swaddled city, puddles splashed silver and orange, knowing with a certainty far beyond your nine years that this is what it meant to be loved.

Canberra

MARK McDERMOTT

K athy and Lou, mother and daughter, sat beside each other in the den, eyes fixed on the television. The screen was bright, the contrast set at too high a setting, and the volume so high that the internal elements of the speakers buzzed as if a bluebottle had taken up residence within. It had seen better days.

Kathy took up a cigarette, struck a match and lit it. She offered the box to Lou.

"I've given up, Ma. They're too dear."

"Good girl."

The signature music of the game show they had been waiting for rattled from the speakers. "Ah good," breathed Kathy.

A luminous man wearing a pin-striped suit peered out from the screen, whirling his arms to stoke up the audience.

"He's handsome Ma, isn't he?"

"He is. Better in real life, I thought."

Kathy took a puff on her cigarette. The presenter was introducing the first contestant, an elderly lady named Val whose voice shook like a leaf on every word. A brief video biography showed a large gaggle of children flocking around Val in an anonymous yard, all declaring her "the best Nan ever".

"That's one god-awful dress that woman's wearing."

Lou laughed in agreement.

"That's one thing you can say Ma – you didn't win but you were well turned out!" Kathy grunted and took another drag.

The show continued, the host posing questions of ever-increasing difficulty to an increasingly energised Val. The finale arrived, where Val was offered a double or nothing question, which in her hyper-excited state she readily agreed to. Fluttering drums and ominous synth sounds added mock suspense.

"Okay Val," the host began, "this is it. For the money … What is the capital of Venezuela?"

"Caracas," muttered Kathy.

On the screen Val's face had drained and she was making fish-like faces into the camera. "Holy Jesus Mam, it's a pity you didn't get asked that question last week!"

"Not as easy as it looks Lou, there's cameras and lights and all there. Very hot and bright. Terrible pressure."

Kathy shifted in her chair. Her face screwed up like crumpled paper. She pushed up her glasses.

"Didn't need the money anyway," she said forthrightly.

Val was clapped off, defeated, setting off another round of fuzzy distortion in the speakers.

"You could've bought a new T.V. for a start," Lou smiled.

"I should've got that question right though. Sydney? Jesus. Everyone knows it's Canberra."

"Ah sure who cares! It was only a bit of fun."

Kathy sat still for a minute, thinking, then her face relaxed.

"True love. We're happy enough, aren't we?"

The show played on. A new contestant sidled up.

"Look at her feckin' makeup Ma! Jesus…"

Winter Birds

KIERAN BYRNE

Sometimes she'd put the bread in the fridge and the milk in the food press. And sometimes, Pat would need to re-visit the boot of the car when his wife, Maggie, had forgotten to bring in a last bag of groceries.

Sometimes, they'd laugh over the stuff she was forgetting. Sometimes Maggie would look at him in mock reproach, her blue eyes alive with mirth, and start clapping her hands together.

'What d'yeh think I am, sealion?' she'd say, and both of them would crack up.

But sometimes she'd be gone, not in body but in mind, for hours at a time. She'd sit in her housecoat, her eyes turning as cold as the forgotten tea he'd made her.

But she'd come back. She always did.

Sometimes she'd say: 'Who are you? What are you doing in my house?' And that's when Pat sat, lonely and heartbroken, with tears stinging his eyes.

But she'd come back. She always did.

Now, as she sat on the sofa, her blue eyes once again clouded in their pouches of sagging skin, Pat looked at the memories on the walls. Himself and Maggie, snapped on Dingle harbour, Maggie rosy-cheeked and laughing, himself impossibly young, his hair impossibly black; himself and Maggie,

caught in grainy black and white on O'Connell Street after seeing 'Whiskey Galore' at the Savoy; himself and Maggie, frozen in mid-step on the dance-floor of the Met Ballroom, Maggie's eyes dancing and happy. Now, they were no spring chickens. More like winter birds. But what a wonderful summer they'd had – one that had lasted nearly fifty years.

Even when Maggie was gone - when the creeping flood of forgetfulness seeped in and washed out the memories – she made up for it when she returned.

She'd come back. She always did.

Pat went to the kitchen, pulled out the second drawer under the worktop, and looked in.

Nothing. Then he remembered. He went to the car and unlocked the boot. Yes. There it was in the forgotten bag, nestling amongst the eggs and the milk and the butter: the Powers Gold Label they'd picked up at the supermarket. Tonight was Classics on the vintage channel.

Pat went back into the sitting-room. The Powers Gold Label bottle caught a flicker of candlelight from the mantel. The light danced across the glass, bright and happy and warm, a symbol of his life with his sweetheart.

Pat poured two glasses and hoisted one high.

'Here's to us, Maggie.' But he didn't take a sip. Not then. Not yet.

Instead he sat beside his wife, kissed her cheek, took her hand in his. And waited.

She'd come back. She always did.

How Are You Feeling Today?

LEAH WILLIAMS

"*H*ow are you feeling today, love?" Sarah asked, placing a hand on her husband's shoulder, squeezing the bone that jutted out between his shoulder blades.

Pat lifted his head. He opened his mouth and moved his jaw, as if chiselling unformed words between his teeth, then he sighed and clasped his lips back together.

"Coffee, love?"

"Please," he croaked, a nerve in his cheek jumping.

He weaved his juddering fingertips together, cradling a cup between his palms.

"Have you taken your tablets?"

"Yes," he nodded.

She smiled at him. Her pupils snagged on his momentarily. He lifted one hand inches away from his body, a pulse of the man he was urging him to reach for his wife. A pinch of the darkness pulled his hand back down again, into the pocket of his dressing gown. Sarah moved away, her scarf trailing behind her as she paced out of the kitchen.

A crash of crockery against wood vibrated through the floorboards. Pat jolted, he shuffled, his ear directed towards the noise. Footsteps spooled through the hall. A fist jangled against the door. Pat clutched the dented doorknob and hauled the door open. Niall gazed upwards and pointed at his chin, dripping with thick white lumps. "Spilled my porridge," he said, his voice several octaves too deep for a four year old.

Pat's blue dressing gown, longer in the front as he slouched forward, flapped against his pale legs, red hairs sticking upwards against the cold. "Here you go," Pat uttered, pulling the tap release up and drenching the corner of a towel beneath the flow of water. He took a step towards his son, his curved back lowering him down to the height of the child.

He dabbed the green material against Niall's pursed mouth, his small eyebrows pulled tight at the top of his nose, eyes scuttling over the lines on his father's face, a face etched of frowns.

"Dad," he said, placing his hand on his father's leg, his voice muffled by the towel.

"Yes son," Pat whispered, his voice barely hatching from the shell of his sadness.

"You're more gently."

"Am I?" Pat uttered, his eyes tilting upwards for the first time in weeks. Tears seeped over his bottom eyelashes.

"Why you sad?" Niall asked, placing a clammy hand on his dad's face.

"I've been a bit sad Niall," Pat sniffed. "I don't really know why."

Niall wriggled his fingers against his father's stubble.

"Dad?" he said, eyes widening.

Pat blinked and sighed; "yes son."

"Will you bring me to the park?"

"Boring old me?"

Niall squashed his other hand against Pat's face, pushing his fingers into a stubbly cheek. "You're not boring dad. You're my favourite."

Frankie & Maggie Together

SUZANNE O'BRIEN

rankie stared out into the garden as the heavy pelts of rain threw themselves against the window. The thought of having to venture out into the storm that surrounded him was daunting, yet inevitable. Outside was waiting for him.

He reached for his gold tie that was draped over the back of the rickety old chair at the bottom of the bed. He fastened it so neatly and so carefully into the nook of his crisp white shirt collar. He looked in the mirror hanging on the back of the door and took pride in his dapper appearance. Only his silver hair gave him away, but for a man of almost eighty, he looked undoubtedly young. He'd had the same boyish twinkle in his eye for nearly 65 years now, ever since the day his sweetheart Maggie had first settled in his heart. Frankie often had difficulty remembering what he had eaten for breakfast that morning, but he could tell you about every second he'd ever spent with Maggie, and given half the chance, he would.

He could remember first meeting her outside St. Joseph's Church when they were fourteen and both avoiding choir practice and the horror that was Father Comerford. He could remember the years that followed, disobeying all mothers, fathers and priests for the chance to hold her hand behind the old stone wall behind Saunders Pub. He could remember the colour of her lips on their wedding day, the smell of her perfume on the day they bought their home, and the saltiness of her tears the day their son Andrew was born. But not only could he remember all this, and more, but he could feel every moment they'd ever shared. It never failed to amaze him that they had built such a beautiful life together. He could see their success every time he looked at his grand-daughter, Ruby, and how she adored and loved her grandmother with every mite in her body. Not if he used every muscle he had, could he be any more proud of all they had together.

Frankie combed his thick head of hair until he considered it perfect. Trying to find the silver lining in the day, he smiled and thought to himself that it was no wonder Maggie had fallen for him.

Andrew's voice could be heard from downstairs telling him it was time to go. Outside was waiting. It was time to go. It was time to say goodbye to his sweetheart. Frankie smiled. He knew that tomorrow he would be sad, that tomorrow he would grieve. But today he planned on celebrating the fact that he had witnessed the most beautiful life he had ever known.

The Letter Writer

MARIE MORAN

I had rehearsed the speech carefully, but now that the time had come, felt naked and ill-prepared. There was no going back, however. I had announced my intention to say something important. He looked at me warily, and shifted uncomfortably in his seat. Flushed with wine and uncertainty, I began. 'You see, the thing is, I think you're great.' Each word felt as foreign and surprising as a pebble in my mouth. 'I like you. I mean, really like you.' I struggled to capture the easy brilliance of those earlier rehearsals, startled by how anaemic and mundane my words sounded outside the theatre of my own perfidious mind. I rushed to cover the four key points I had agreed with myself before he could intervene, resisting the urge to count them off on my fingers as I proceeded. 'I like the way you think.' Abandoned now by both poetry and empirical evidence, I continued doggedly. 'I like how you treat people. You make me laugh. I'm attracted to you.' And then finally, inevitably – 'I think I'm in love with you.' The couple at the table next to us paused momentarily in their conversation, and a stillness descended. It seemed to me as though the entire room held its breath.

Time doesn't behave as it ought. In the moments between my declaration and the forthcoming – surely, forthcoming – response, I returned once more to that theatre of my mind, and was flooded with memories spanning years. An old ache, throbbing with forgotten intensity, revisits.

I turn again to look at it, drink in the smell of his skin, and run my fingers greedily along the curve of his arm. Remembering him, though, this time,

I remembered myself: I remembered the letter writer. Hastily scribbled directives, delivered with the clarity of a prisoner on death row, then hidden furtively for later stumbling across where they are received in shock as though written by another, interfering person. Nonetheless, a single author, a single reader, a single message: leave him. Find yourself.

There are only so many letters you can ignore. I found that was possible to love and to leave, to lose and to find, at the same time. And so I continued, slowly, unevenly, until pebble words have replaced frantic script, and I find myself here, outside a busy Dublin restaurant, recounting what it is that I want to someone who doesn't want it back.

'Thank you,' he said, 'but I'm with somebody.' Of course, I knew that, had known that before I'd even begun. Choosing without being chosen is bittersweet, but I felt it as a quiet victory. I smiled, lit a cigarette and thought about giving them up.

Dear Sir with Love

ANTHONY McDONNELL

*H*arold caught his reflection in the panelled glass on the dividing doors to the living room, the winter sun allowing a clear image. A forehead that was blotchy and bumpy, lines on his pug face etched a life of many years worked to the bone by his office masters. Strained grey hairs journeyed across a barren fleshy landscape, not quite arriving at their destination.

"Christ what happened to me?" he smiled to his mirror image. Yet he never felt so young and vital. Harold thought of his 47 years spent on this planet, in this house and what he had achieved, a wife, some good friends, no real enemies. A good man for sure, but never perfect. He had always set out to do his best but like most, being the best that you could be, occurred as often as a sighting of Halley's Comet.

"Dear Sir, we have not received payment...,"

"Dear Sir, you are 3 months overdue ...,"

"Dear Sir, we regret to inform you that your service has been disconnected."

"Dear Sir" "Dear Sir" "Dear Sir".

"How polite they are, when twisting the knife," thought Harold.

"Dear Sir, we regret to inform you that you have been deemed inadequate by society and so are due for castration in two weeks' time, please contact us to confirm the appointment," Harold thought to himself.

Six months ago he was given the news by his section manager that his job was redundant, not him he was assured. He had trained the little fecker in. A job he had done for 20 years, he did not love it, but he did not hate it either. Over time it had become an acquired taste. In recent years it had come to define part of his existence, it was his main purpose in life as he saw it then. The worry was, what was he going to do at his age, in this economic climate and how in hell was he going tell Nessa? How were they going to pay the bills? They were over extended already. Harold smiled at the memory.

Nessa walked in and put her jacket on, Harold moved to put his on, but just before he did, he slid out a letter from the middle drawer of the desk, opened it carefully and skipped to the key words: "Dear Sir, Results of your recent test.......benign."

Harold pushed the bills and letters into the corner, Nessa looked at him, no words just a warm loving look and a smile that made him fall in love with her all over again.

Pictures, No Sound

PETER NUGENT

When he goes out, and she's in bed, I've taken to looking through their old wedding photos. They honeymooned at his aunt's guesthouse in Dublin. When my mother's memory was good she told me that on their wedding night they prayed. Not like me, then.

She knew the seed, breed and generation of our street, now nothing. I said as much to him. Something has to be done. She is even refusing a visit from her priest. He jarred on the words "her priest". I was sharp with him.

"I am your carer, it's my responsibility to look after you both."

He spat back. "And I am her husband. He couldn't stop. "Look at you, you can barely look after yourself, never mind us."

That set me off.

He found me this morning under her good coat on the sofa. It's been pictures, no sound from him. And then to make a point he brought her down and sat her next to me in the kitchen. This is how it's done, look and learn, daughter. He got scissors from under the sink and cut her nails.

He made some tea (I wasn't offered any) and as a treat, stood her next to the window. Backs to me, they watched blackbirds eat bread from the roof of the coal shed. Without looking round his lordship commanded that I run a bath for her. I did as I was told and left clean underwear and clothes in the bathroom. We ushered her upstairs and I let him undress her. "Now's your chance," he said. "Get into her room and make her bed while she's in the bath."

I changed the sheets and listened out for her (the walls are like paper). I listened as she got dressed and opened the door. I expected her to jump straight back into her bed but, as I told him just now, I got the surprise of my life when for the first time in ages she turned on the landing and waltzed back downstairs to him in the kitchen. I told him he had the magic touch.

This time he offered me a cup of his tea. After a while he moved her to the window and then sotto voce mouthed at me to stand between them. We held each other's' hands and together looked out at the blackbirds on the coal shed roof, no sounds, just pictures and pictures of birds, and of me stretching out the moment, a celebration.

The Best Heart

MARY KATE O FLANAGAN

*H*is parents met us at the airport. I was a little shy of course, because I didn't know them. So I hung back when they waved and even hopped with excitement and held their arms out. He kissed his mother hello. And then he kissed his father. Like a little boy. I knew he wanted to marry me and I thought, I can't marry this little boy. And then he turned and put his arm around me and they hugged me too and it was so kind and a little too hot in that embrace. They wanted me to make their little boy happy and I doubted that I would.

And then we went to their house and all his older brothers were waiting for us and of course their wives and the children. They treated me like I was one of the family already and it was so noisy and too warm.

I pretended to want to see the garden just for some peace and fresh air and he walked with me. In the half-darkness he said to me, "You thought it was strange when I kissed my father, didn't you?" He took my hand and he said, "It's not easy to be the youngest of six boys. You're never the biggest or the fastest or the cleverest and you always want to be more grown-up than you are. When I was ten, I realised that I was the only one of us who kissed my father goodnight. The others kissed my mother goodnight and just nodded at my Dad. Once I realised, I saw how babyish it is for a boy to kiss his Daddy like that. So I thought, I'll stop. That night, I could hardly bring myself to say goodnight. My heart was heavy and I felt tight in my throat. I was announcing my adulthood to my parents. There they sat; reading side by side on the sofa, little knowing what a big night this was for me. Eventually, I stood up and I walked over and kissed my mother and said good night. My father looked up smiling and I put my hands in my pockets, nodded at him and said, Goodnight. Just like my brothers did. His face never changed. He smiled steadily and said, Goodnight. I thought perhaps he hadn't even noticed the change in our routine. I was a little surprised. So as I closed the door, I glanced back in and I saw them look at each other for a long moment. He said to her, 'I've lost the last one'. So I walked back into that room and I kissed my Dad goodnight and I always will. Even if it looks silly."

And I looked at him in the half-light and I thought, I must marry this man.

Are You My Girl?

ANNE LUNDON

Are you my girl?

As I dug the springtime earth to plant the new beginnings the frog appeared. He darted out of the way of my shovel. He had luck on his side. He could have been split open. I slacken my pace and look out for him. I am conscious of harming the frog. There is life there so I must be careful. I muse as what his tiny brain is processing. Is he wondering why the earth has moved?

What made her earth move to make her feel so sad? I wonder if she has come back to keep me company as a frog. Is she diverting me from the knife of pain that carves my heart? If I kissed this frog would my princess return? My girl was beautiful but so sad. Because she was sad people saw the frog and could not see the beauty. How come she did not have that luck? Was her life slashed because of destiny or disdain?

Maybe she is the blackbird or the robin? Where is her song? Her singing touched hearts. She was greatly loved and she loved greatly. She celebrated birthdays but she could not see that we cannot celebrate death. When her great brain was tired where were the trained brains to help her mend? When she was spotted to be in danger why did their pace to save her not accelerate and she not even a frog!

They say frogs are ugly. I like their slimy skin and observing eyes in a comical body that can leap from dangers to avoid being sliced. She did not have the layer of thick skin that might have buoyed her on this earth. Did she not matter enough to mind her when we left her in your care? Their croaks are easy listening. Her "croaking" has left life severed. Life is in two halves. One half was with her the other is without.

At close of day the frog hops home for the night. Then I spot a smaller frog camouflaged in the grass. I wonder if it is going to be reunited with its parent only a few feet away! Will they celebrate meeting up at the end of yet another day within the confines of the garden? Would her children have played in my garden?

My heart lifts and heals a little because she will never have to feel this pain of losing her child. She is in a place where her spirit is roaming free. She is in my being. I carry her with me. I will plant the seeds tomorrow. The digging is over. I will celebrate the new growth and feel her presence in my garden of life.

Through a Pane of Glass

ANNE FARRELL

I like watching birds. Birds are like people but with one huge advantage. They can fly. Most mornings, at about eleven, I look at my resident robin through the kitchen window. Often, he is perched on the corner of the triangular clothesline. He seems to stare back at me, a look of defiance in those ever-vigilant eyes. He is a wary, knowing bird.

This morning, I spend longer than usual watching. I am waiting for an important phone call. You can learn a lot about birds by just watching them in a small garden. For instance, people think that robins are cocky and intrepid birds but I think that they just put up a very brave front.

There's a lot of competition out there in a small garden. Hanging from the birch tree are two feeders and only so much food to go around. The narrow wire mesh is designed to discourage the bigger more aggressive birds from encroaching, but it doesn't stop starlings. There are so many, and a feeder can be emptied pretty fast. That's just the way it is. Starlings are fine-feathered birds.

There are many tits in the garden. Blue tits, Great tits, Coal tits … I could go on. They are clever birds. They hide until the big birds have had their fill and gradually reappear when it is safe. They gather in groups for protection and manage to feed well. If they were people they would form a Union. They could call themselves TWIT (Tit Workers of Ireland). You have to laugh, don't you?

It's mid-April and, despite the frosty weather, the garden is slowly stirring. Although there are no leaves on the birch tree yet, strange-looking seeds droop in abundance. The small birds tenaciously cling on to the feeders swaying in the breeze. An occasional blackbird hops around the ground seeking out worms. Like the robin, he seems a bit of a loner. I suppose it runs in the family. Chaffinches, Greenfinches, and Bullfinches fly from branch to branch, a law unto themselves. A few down-at-heel sparrows try to assert themselves.

Suddenly, the inhabitants ascend in all directions. A lone magpie swoops and lands, magnificent in black and white, staring about him like a storm trooper. Surveying the deserted garden and the protected food, he sweeps off in disgust.

The phone makes me jump. I answer with trepidation. The long pause confirms my fears. "The bank said no." His voice is weary. I sigh, inaudibly.

"We'll be ok. "

"Sure, sure. Gotta go. Talk later." He hangs up.

The small birds have returned. My robin stares defiantly from the ground. I will miss my tree.

Pink

FIONA NALLY

hen I think back on that day, I could have sworn the bone marrow I received, was pink. In my head, I still have a vivid memory of looking up at the bag I was connected to and finding the colour vaguely reassuring at the time. During the previous year, I had been receiving red blood cells and cream coloured platelets and it made some kind of sense to me that the marrow might be between the two. Except, it turns out that it wasn't. This was a life-changing moment for me and I've remembered it wrong.

My sister was my witness to my big moment. It took some time before I was ready to talk to her about that day. For months post-transplant, I couldn't speak at all about what I had gone through while I was in the hospital. As my recovery progressed however, I started to want to piece together the jumble of memories I did have, into some kind of order. When I finally asked her, it turned out the marrow I remembered as pink, was in fact a creamy colour quite similar to platelets. How could I have remembered this detail wrong? If you asked me to close my eyes and think back, I can still picture that pale pink.

All in all, I was pretty naïve entering the hospital for the transplant. I had been talked to about my survival odds, what could go wrong and various medical details. But I was not prepared at all. I thought once the actual transplant was completed that I'd just spend a few weeks getting better and emerge from hospital, having kept daily records of my life changing experience. I'd imagined maybe even posting a daily blog and writing up a memoir during my recovery. Not quite.

I was a lot sicker than was anticipated. In fact, I am lucky to be here to write this. I've been torn down by illness, rebuilt and reborn. I have been given a second chance at life. If I can't fully remember exactly what I went through, I believe that's self-preservation. My own recollection of what I went through is jumbled and out of sequence. It's funny how the memory of pain fades into the tapestry of life lived.

The memories may be hazy but what matters is that I have prevailed. I have come through a life changing experience and I can take stock of what I have. If I can't remember the finer details, I remember the love and support that carried me through. The past fades and it's each new day that counts.

What Matters

GERALDINE MILLS

my hoodie is no match for the cold that stalks me along the street as I make my way home from the football pitch. Before I even get to our house I can make out the shape of dad sitting on the doorstep. Up close, he's shivering. I sit down beside him as near as I can without touching him. Stars explode and disappear into black holes in the time it takes him to speak.

"My job's gone, son. After twenty years. Just gone." I don't know what to say to him so I stuff my hands further into my pockets. "How am I going to tell your mother?"

And his voice sort of trickles down the plughole of the dark. We sit there for a while watching the light fall from the street lamps and night creep out from under the hedge that divides us and the neighbours. I begin to shiver too. If we stay out any longer we'll be turned into pillars of chill. I crouch down in front of the door, push open the letterbox and shout through its gaping mouth.

"Mam, it's me. Let us in."

I have to call a few times before I hear her squeaking along the hall in her baskety sandals, the only ones that will fit her swollen feet. 'Puffer-fish feet' she calls them. She opens the door.

"At last," she says, looking from one to the other of us. "Ye were gone so long, I thought I had lost ye. And what would I do then without my two precious men?" She puts her hand on dad's shoulder. She knows. He doesn't have to tell her anything. I watch him walk by her, without saying a thing, through the house and out into the yard. She follows him. Out there, she stands close to him, looking up into his face, talking. I cannot hear a word she says because it's drowned out by the wind-clap of wings as the pigeons come flying down from the roof. They've been waiting for him too.

"We've managed before," I finally hear her say, "and we'll manage again. Now I'll go in and cook you your favourite." She touches his cheek before heading back into the kitchen. Soon there's a great smell of frying.

The pigeons are all around dad, their plumage puffed out, their tails fanned. Some of them have beautiful wing patches, shining in the evening light, a pink iridescent sheen as they peck away. Dad stands there, a look on his face like he isn't worried that his job is gone or anything; like he's seeing the gates of heaven open before him.

Perfect Fit

DEIRDRE NALLY

No one could quite understand why the handsome prince had changed his mind and married the ugly sister, who was overweight and smoked like a trooper. Especially when he could have had the beautiful princess who had hair like spun gold and skin like a dew soaked peach. Even the princess could not understand how this had happened. There was no one in the land more beautiful than her and certainly no one who had gone to as much trouble to make their wedding day the most perfect day of their life. No one who had spent so many weeks going to wedding fairs and bridal shops and stationery outlets; selecting, comparing, sampling and trying on. No one who had spent so many nights drawing up lists of what their heart desired in order that they could live happily ever after with their handsome prince and with all the expensive tableware and coffee makers and matching luggage they could ever want.

"It's the wrong shade of turquoise," she had said as the cake maker presented her with ribbons that matched the groom's tie and cummerbund. "They just don't look right," she had frowned as the floral arrangements for the tables were set before her. "You'll have to lose weight," she had ordered the bridesmaids who twirled in front of her seeking royal approval.

The handsome prince watched her, growing sadder and lonelier as the beautiful princess spent all her time planning their very special day. "I don't even know what a Nespresso machine is. Why do I need a Nespresso machine?" he said as he glared at the wedding list and the ugly sister laughed and offered him a drag of her cigarette.

"Chair covers. Hundreds of bloody euro for linen chair covers," he despaired and she patted his shoulder and bought him another pint. "They're flowers, they're just bloody flowers" he almost sobbed and she hugged him tightly and quickly.

There came the day that the beautiful princess discovered that the handsome prince had forgotten to book the vintage white Rolls and they would have to make do with the black limousine. She ranted, she raved, she stamped her feet and she burst into loud furious sobs. The handsome prince looked at her and he saw; he saw her false gilded hair and her fake gold tanned skin, her angry glossed lips and her hard blood red nails. He kissed the ugly sister and finally awoke from his deep sleep.

At their wedding, the Fiat broke down on the way to the church, the singer forgot to turn up, and the ugly sister wore runners because her glass slippers were killing her. And they all lived happily ever after.

Chips

CJ SCUFFINS

Terry walked into the front room, where I was watching some stupid puppet yokes on the telly with my big brother Ian, who we called Iano for short. Iano had warned me. He said Terry would try to be nice, 'cause he wanted to get into Ma's pants'. I thought that was just wrong. Did he not have pants of his own?

"Are you coming down the Rovers with me, lads?" asked Terry.

Iano kept his eyes on the telly and said nothing.

"No," I goes. "We're watching these puppet yokes. They're deadly."

"They don't look deadly."

"They're better than Shamrock Rovers, that's for sure." Iano kept saying nothing, but I could tell that he liked that one.

"Grand, so," said Terry. He turned to the door – and then turned back. "Oh, by the way, do you like chips?"

Iano flinched.

"Why?" I goes. I didn't know what class of trick he was trying to pull here, but you should never mess-talk about chips. "Do they have a van at Rovers?"

"Yep," Terry said.

"When are we going?" I said.

"We're going now. You coming or what, Ian?"

Iano still didn't look up. But he did speak. Quietly, with determination. A bit like that granddad off the telly, Clint Eastwood. "What chipper is in the ground? Macari's, I bet."

Iano tutted. It was like a firecracker going off in some oul' wan's letterbox. Macari's was an Italian chipper in Tallaght's main street. It was run by a bunch of Chinese girls.

"Burdock's," Terry goes. "The best Burdock's in Dublin."

Iano jumped up and stepped to him. He was the estate's leading expert on chips. And his gander was up.

"What are you talking about? The best Burdock's is in town, around the corner from that church."

"Christ Church?" said Terry.

"The one at the back of Burdock's," said Iano, losing patience now.

"So, you've had chips out of that Burdock's, then?" said Terry.

"Only every single birthday."

"Did they put on the salt and vinegar for you?"

"Course they did. And plenty of it."

"The Burdock's in Tolka doesn't."

"No salt and vinegar?"

Iano's sneer stretched from eyebrow to kneecap. Terry just stood there, staring at the stupid puppets on the telly. Like a sap. Then he looked at the pair of us again. A big pearler on his mush.

"You do the salt and vinegar yourself!"

I was sitting in the back of the car before Iano's jaw hit the floor. This Terry fella was welcome to Ma's pants, her blouses and her scarves, as far as I was cared. On the way to the ground, Iano didn't say a single word. Shock, doctors called it.

Word made Flesh

ORLA GLEESON

I was informed coolly by the nursing manager that it was my problem now. The child (deceased) was anacephalic. As the pregnancy was below a certain time threshold, the child had to be delivered, not by the midwifery service but by a staff nurse on a Surgical ward.

"Anacephalic" - a melodious word, exotic and logical. A word that belied the bleakness of its meaning, that of lacking a cerebral hemisphere. Headless. A brutal deformity. I shuddered inwardly for the mother and child.

I was aware of turned backs, shoes clicking on the polished floors, a certain managerial satisfaction at a problem jettisoned. I was newly qualified as a nurse. I had never delivered a baby and certainly not a dead one. I took one breath and then another. I knew the cool marble facts of the situation. But I knew that there was something else too: an unwillingness to look at this dead child, a fear of monsters and misshapen things, for do we not associate beauty and goodness with symmetry, balance, fullness and health?

I sent away the student nurse who was working with me. She was a mirror of my own feelings of incompetence, of dread. I need not have worried. The woman was already a mother to three children. She had accepted the sadness of the loss of this child, the little one that we delivered into the world between us two hours later. Scarlet red on the bright white sheet.

When I first saw her, I felt something breaking in my head, a recognition, something that the mother had known all along. Imperfect, yet perfect. The back of her head was flat when it should have been round and full but her face was like that of a small red doll. Her eyes were closed. Her features tiny and even. Her hands had sought each other and were joined as though in prayer. As I laid her out in the white doll's dress that her mother had brought with her, I realised that she was a very beautiful little soul whose time had not yet come.

The student nurse hovered beyond the room. When I came out, she asked, almost gulping in horror, "was it, are you...?"

"Would you like to see her?" I asked.

Later, she said to me "I am glad I looked. I am glad that I saw.." I nodded in agreement. "I am so glad I looked. I thought ...you see, I thought..."

"So did I," I said.

The Egg

ROBERT FANNIN

*T*here was something in Eamon's egg. Something curled, like a tiny roll of carpet in the yoke. He used his fork to get it out. It was a piece of paper. Paper! He uncurled it. There were words, 'Die Mouse - Gold Cup', it said.

He looked up. The cafe was empty but for the usual two or three, Dolan studying form over his empty plate, the others silhouetted against steamed-up winter windows. It could be a horse, Eamon thought. Dolan might know. I could ask. No! He thinks I'm nuts. But on the way out Eamon caught Dolan's eye.

"'Eh, hello. By the way I think I might know who's going to win the Gold Cup."

Dolan stared up at him, "Wha?"

"I think I might know who's going to win the Gold Cup."

"The Gold Cup?"

"Yeah!"

"Listen son the Gold Cup doesn't run 'till March."

"Oh!"

"Unless you mean the Melbourne Gold Cup?"

Eamon brightened, "When does that run?"

Dolan studied him, "Tomorrow."

"Is a horse called Die Mouse running?"

"Die Mouse! You must be joking! Die Mouse was shipped to Australia years ago and as far as I know ended up as dog food."

Eamon nodded towards the paper, "Can you check?"

Dolan shook his head and looked back at the page. "I'm telling you," he said. Then his eyebrows lifted. "Well, according to this she's running, but I'll tell you, you'd want to be a right gobshite to put money down on that."

Back in his flat Eamon filled a bag with anything he thought might have value, including two cameras that a friend had asked him to look after years before and who Eamon hadn't heard a word from since. He got fifty euro at the pawn shop and went straight to the bookie.

"Die Mouse to win please," he said to the blank faced woman up behind the counter.

When he took the top off his egg the following morning there was another rolled up piece of paper catching the neon in the yellow yoke. He looked up at the sound of the door slamming and saw Dolan marching straight for him.

"How did you know?" He was livid.

"Did it win?"

"Fifty to bloody one!" His eyes were wild. "How did you know?"

"Eh, the egg..." Eamon said pointing.

Dolan leaned forward. "To hell with the bloody egg! I want to know how you knew." He waited. When Eamon didn't say anything Dolan straightened, swung on his heels and stormed to his table.

Fifty euro at fifty to one was...his mind raced, two thousand, five hundred Euro! Again, using his fork, he pulled out the piece of paper and uncurled it. It read, "Tell that bastard nothing."

Together

ARIEL DI VEROLI SILVERA

The bright living room lights contrast the pitch black night beyond the windows. How long have we been together today? Nine, ten hours maybe?

Johnny isn't happy, for he knows what's coming as Siobhan hands him the card. Taking the putty in his hands, he sets to work. His teammates have 30 seconds to guess the word, based on Johnny's work of sculptural art. His brow furrows, as he clumsily starts kneading the green, sticky mass. I smile across the room at Siobhan as she stifles a giggle in agreement. They haven't a chance.

As the seconds tick away, I see Maria is still at work on the newcomer, Christie, as she has been doing sporadically throughout the day. Christie smiles a lot but is quiet, fighting the good fight against American stereotypes. We met her at the parade, and Maria took an instant liking to her dishevelled short hair and 80s rocker denim jacket.

Every year is like this, the same core group, the same family members. But there's always some new, lone soul to refresh the spirit of the proceedings. Which is merciful on Ciaran, who is tired of hearing the very hilarious story of when I fell from a boat that one time, or about Johnny's romantic woes, or all of our stories we all know inside out.

"It's a deer!" Sean has lit up, after having his chin buried well within his hand in concentration.

The seconds are ticking away, and Johnny shakes his head quickly, the putty moulded into something resembling a serpent with horns. Time.

I move to the kitchen, because all of a sudden I want to give Ciaran a big hug. He's standing in the doorway having a smoke, blonde hair falling across his face. He looks lost in thought but notices me as I close the door behind me, blocking the chaos inside. I hold him, feeling just how tense his back is.

"Having a good smoke, hun?" I ask.

"Hmm, sorta. It's just, you know, big shouty group in a small space, you know how I get."

I smile, because I know what he means. For me, though, this time of the year is the true Christmas. And it's not that he doesn't love it, he loves seeing everyone in one place, but he needs his alone time. He puts out his ciggie, strokes my beard and kisses my cheek. "Wanna come to the shop with me? I'm out of tobacco," he says. In this evening light, he almost glows.

"Sure," I say, holding his hand.

The Devil's Thumb

MICHELE FORBES

On his forty-seventh climb he had conquered the southern face of The Devil's Thumb. He had recorded his exultation in his beloved frost-frayed notebook. The day after he arrived home he had fallen over the dog. The wallop of his skull against the dolce latte marble tiles of his kitchen floor bore nothing for forty eight hours, despite his vigilant anticipation. Then during an episode of CSI: Miami he had softly rolled off the sofa into a croissant shaped coma. Freshly delivered on a hospital trolley he was welcomed by a cluster of sceptical but interested consultants - since he too was a doctor - and the diagnosis had been grim. The blood cloud, which had by now saturated the galleries of his neo-cortex for forty nine hours, had apparently haemorrhaged away fifty years of his life, more or less.

Now upon waking, fifty one days later, his memories have separated into tiny cellular prisms, some operative, some not. Occasionally the fat of his brain pops and something surfaces but he does not understand its significance nor feel the ring of familiarity. What he does know is that now he lives in a terrifying white present. A nurse jostles his drip like a curtain cord. A woman who claims to be his wife hands him a frost-frayed notebook. "Read this Eamon," she says gently, her gaze like pressed orchids, "and come out from under the devil's thumb." She kisses him on the mouth. He stares at her saying to himself I hope I love you.

As he reads he learns that his now bruised soul had something amazing to compare itself with. Fifteen years ago it was Elbrus - the jewel of the Caucasus

- and after that Chogori, then Mount Khuiten. On airless Annapurna he had pitched tent before the moon switched on. The weather catapulting at an alarming pace against the glacial streaked peaks. The night a hell's shudder. Though frightened he had trusted his resilience and his fear and had slept like a baby through the storm and in the morning had found an avalanche one metre away from his tent. So, it had happened before the book tells him, every landmark in his life had once before been wiped out in one blissful spread of snow.

He looks at the woman who claims to be his wife. I can remember that I burnt my tongue on the hospital soup, he says to her, but I can't remember the names of my children or what they look like. She lifts her head to the doorway. As he turns three beautiful young men come in to see him. He feels a lost domain expanding his veins.

Remember Me

ESTHER GREENFIELD

S he sits alone and has been doing so for years. The dust collects and the clock ticks on. She waits. She waits for the phone to ring, waits to be moved from her home, waits to return to him.

She can't move so well now. Her back aches, her legs are stiff and unsteady. Her hands can hardly grip her mug of tea. She wonders if it is guilt that keeps her daughter away? Is it frustration that stops her from calling? Or is it impatience? She doesn't enjoy days like this. Lucid thoughts and memories that she can't share. Does she enjoy the days that she can't remember?She thinks about him a lot now. She had coped well after his death. She was younger, busier, still had a life to live. Now nothing, only a longing for the numbness and confusion to end.

She glances at the photos on the mantelpiece. Smiling, young and happy. Him, her, their daughter. She struggles to recognise them. She's unsure of where it was taken. A very long time ago.

Did her daughter visit and did she just forget? Did it really matter? If her daughter visited and she wasn't 'there', did her daughter really visit? She looks around the room. It is familiar to her. The books that she once read. The paintings she once admired. The ornaments she had once collected.

She drives home with tears in her eyes. She has witnessed her mother deteriorate for the past two years. The visits hadn't become any easier. Every day she returns home and clutches her own daughter tightly. She never wants to forget these moments. Never wants to become a stranger.

She desperately completes the weekly crossword. A vain attempt at training her brain to remember. Deep down she knows it won't work. Her parents enjoyed a crossword. She had hoped that filling her mother's room at the home with the familiar would keep her with them for longer. It had made no difference. When she looks into her mother's eyes, there is no recognition. She could be anyone. It didn't matter though. She pulls into her driveway and dries her eyes. She will return tomorrow. Always a vague hope of catching a glimpse of the woman who had encouraged and cared for her.

As she turns the key in the lock she smiles to herself. The only thing that mattered was that she had been loved and would continue to love.

The Kiss

LOUISE BYRNE

The small country school looks extra welcoming on that first sunny day back after Easter break. The plants, grown and maintained by the children, are in late April health and colour. Some are resting, gathering energy for a future time, others readying themselves for a full, flaming shot of summer glory.

An anxious dark haired mother hurries her bespectacled junior from a car, parked askew in the near empty yard. An empty wrapper swirls its escape from the open car door before mother and child swiftly track and capture it. They run together, giggling towards the school door. Junior's unexpected and comic mimicking of a passing parent dissolves her mother's anxiety. Hilarity ensues. Their race to the cloakroom is a draw. They arrive in a jumble of bouncing pink school bag, air-gasping, coat holding, pulling and puffing.

They hush their exuberant voices in the sudden quietness of the bright corridor and make mock shocked wide eyes at each other.

"I won!" the mother says suddenly, prodding Junior in the bum. This produces a loud, echoing squeal. Immediately, they both hunch over, index fingers touching their lips, eyes widened now with mock terror and control battling to manage their joint mischief.

Junior's small coat is hung on a low rail of jumbled ballerina pinks and superhero navies. Her Tinkerbell lunch box is placed reverently beside

Spiderman. Behind the glasses, her eyes gleam excitedly as she tiptoes herself up to assess the waiting classroom scene.

One still somewhat chubby hand, reaches for the classroom door, the other blindly searches for her mother. Junior half turns. "I'll miss you Mom. See you later. Mwah! Mwah!"

The mother, with full accuracy and speed of a heat seeking missile, locates and pulls the searching hand towards her. "Give me a kiss, you fart and you can have some of my lipstick…" is answered immediately with a full frontal vision of small and shaking, breakfast marked, wet lips. The kiss is honey-sweet, sunny and stolen before the mother has even finished anticipating it.

"I'll miss you too ……." is dissolved by the pure, raw, energy buzz of 31 infants as Junior releases the handle. On the opposite side of the door now, she turns fully towards her mother, rewarding the uncertain wait with a silly, aping smile and a slightly self-conscious downward fluttering wave.

The mother walks back to her car. Silence surrounds her lowered head on the return trip. Amid the resting and readying plants, she feels the flush of immeasurable gratitude blending with a sudden, overpowering loss in the now empty yard.

The Train Back

JIM MULLARKEY

This geyser opposite me in shades, not a word, so I offer him a can and he turns his head, very polite, and says thank you very much, but his stomach wasn't great, and then I says, "There's not much to look at out the window."

"Do you not think so?"

"Sure what could you do out in that muck?"

His jaw smiles. "What about ploughed fields," he says slowly, "and white flowers on black thorn and golden furze?"

I wasn't sure if he was taking the piss out of me.

"My name is Joey," he says and he sticks out his hand. "Are you going to Galway?"

I just says, "Yeah," without thinking about it.

And then the voice in the ceiling squeaked about the next stop and Joey says, "Sixmilebridge. Horse country, my mother used to say."

"It still is" I says because I could see two grey fellas poking about for a blade of grass. After a bit he points behind him and asks if that toilet was vacant and then he gets up, very ginger, and he feels his way down the aisle and that's when I twigged him, and my thoughts came to a full stop.

When he returns he asks me what I see out the window now. And I says, "Just weeds and nothing else and a line of gravel and a hill with trees growing on top of it."

"What kind of trees?"

"Spikey ones."

"Do you know what made those hills and hollows?"

I didn't care what made them but I still said, "What?"

"Glaciers, a long time ago."

I says, "How do you know that?" Just looking at him with my mouth open.

"You mean the ice age?"

"How do you know all that stuff?"

He smiles and says, "My mother used to describe everything she saw, like a story, and then I read about it myself," and he raised his hands as if he had eyes in them.

And all you could see was street lamps by the time we got to Ennis and he links my arm to find out from the man standing on the platform we'll be staying on the same train anyway.

Then I says for the crack, "Where does the light go to in the dark?"

"Light needs a constant source," says he, "like a light bulb or the sun."

I don't know why I asked.

Talk

PATRICIA COBEY

*A*fter the mother had died, the father hoped they could talk, but the daughter turned away.

"I don't want to talk about Mom."

It had been a foreign divorce, but he knew where to get the records. He flew over and back and wondered what he would say about those old, old days while he watched the sea below stretch grey and wrinkled like an elephant hide.

They sat in her boxy living room, the father with a folder of papers on his lap. "Juan. Who?"

Then he simply told her of Juan: the suddenness of attraction, the amazement, their madness, the uproar and gossip, their de-camping to Madrid, the return, the mother cool, people looking the other way, and his suddenly having no place to live, the door closed, scandal from beginning to end.

You mean you and Juan were lovers?

"I wanted to tell you myself, but you knew, didn't you?"

"How would I know? I was just a kid"

She was lying.

Later, she said she remembered how Juan would play cards with her for hours and hours, while he, the father, didn't have any patience. That night the father thought of betrayal. Not his or the mother's but her's. Her not wanting to talk because of a sense of her betraying her mother.

A week later, she telephoned and said he'd left a folder behind.

"I found something."

"What?"

"A declaration Mom made when she applied for the divorce."

"Oh."

"She always said you divorced her. Went off and divorced her."

"I thought that might be the case."

"Why would she say that?"

"Respectable Catholics didn't get divorced back then."

"Why did she then?"

"Peter."

"You mean you were both having affairs?"

"They were an item long before I met Juan."

"You people!"

"We weren't saints."

And that was that. For the rest of the evening she called him Da-aaaad, larding the last syllable with a mock sarcasm that at moments felt real. Then, at the door: "What happened to Juan?"

"Went back to Spain."

She sighed. "And Peter hung in."

"They both hung in."

In Spring the following year, she announced her engagement. She hadn't called for months and months.

"You know, you two were morons."

"Probably."

"And I'm no different. I'm getting married."

"When?"

"Six weeks."

"Am I invited?"

"Yeah."

"You know, it's ok. He was Mom's excuse. A kind of gift."

"That's true. A gift called Juan."

JOHN FITZGERALD

I got back to the ragged and run-down youth hostel at tea time, hungry and cold after another useless, frustrating, wasted day searching for a job.

I went downstairs to the canteen and looked for the cheapest meal I could find; my miserable cash reserves were disappearing rapidly. I took a main course, minced meat, paid for it and went to a table.

A few other residents were scattered about the grim room, looking lonely and lost. Few spoke and when they did the accents were unfamiliar.

As I was about to eat I remembered it was Friday; no meat for me today! I went back to the cashier, a middle-aged woman who looked tired and vexed. I said, "Can I change this for fish please".

"You can't change a meal once it's been at the table. That's the rule," she said dismissively in a cockney accent I could barely understand.

"Oh I'm sorry, I didn't know,"" I replied, flustered and embarrassed. I went back to the table leaving the dish on the counter. I got a coffee which came free from a dispenser and sat, head in hands, thinking of the meal my mother would be putting on the table just about now. Even though it was Friday there would be plenty of spuds, lots of butter and a whole lot more besides.

I could picture my father sitting by the fire, in mellow good humour, carefully nursing his first Powers of the night. The sense of loneliness and loss that had been building inside me since I left home less than a week before intensified. I wanted to be back there - but I couldn't go back until I had made something of myself. And there seemed to be little prospect of doing that in this cold, strange, godforsaken place. I was close to tears.

Then I heard a voice in my ear. The cashier was at my side. "Are you a Catholic," she asked in little more than a whisper. She pronounced it 'cafflick' so it took a second or two to register with me. I nodded in reply, wordless in my misery.

She went to the counter and returned with an oversized plate loaded with fish, set it on the table before me, patted me gently on the shoulder and was gone.

My pit of despair slowly dissolved into a wellspring of hope. This time, the tears were unstoppable.

Danny

CAELAINN BRADLEY

There are some days that stay gold in your memory, even after half a century has passed. I turned eighty-five last week; my once bright-blue eyes are a tired grey and the lines in my face tell the story of the long years I've lived. But I can still remember walking on the beach at Howth with Danny O'Brien in the summer heat. That was 1950, and I can still recall the sun-warmed rocks beneath my bare feet, and the feeling when he took my hand in his.

There are dark memories, too. My father's death. The tears in my mother's eyes as she told me she was moving the family to England. "Kitty, I have to," she said, desperately, "please understand, there's no work for me here. I've no choice..." I'd never seen her cry before. Frightened, I pushed her away and ran out of the house. I sprinted to the beach and out across the sand and when I reached the roaring grey waves, with seagulls crying overhead, I screamed - at the top of my lungs, screaming out all my frustration at the sky and the sea. I won't go, I thought wildly. I'm not leaving Ireland, I'm not leaving Danny, I'm not leaving.

I left. My mother had three children under twelve. She couldn't cope. Danny begged me not to - I was eighteen, old enough to marry him, stay, PLEASE. When I wouldn't, he was so angry he wouldn't even say goodbye. Now, I see an old woman staring back at me from the mirror. But I still remember with startling clarity those warm summer evenings we spent drinking whiskey and watching sunsets. Feeling like nothing could be better than here and now. 62 years ago. I sigh. A sudden shout brings me back from my reverie.

"Kitty?"

"Coming now, Danny!" I reply.

It was during one of my visits home to Ireland; our chance meeting. Both in our sixties – myself widowed, and he divorced - we were bewildered to speak again after so long. But once we started talking, the years fell away. We spent the week together, never running out of things to say.

The day I left, he said, "Kitty, I'm going to do what I should've done forty-three years ago. I'm going to follow you to England, and marry you. If you'll have me."

Now we spend our nights at home, nestled together on the sofa, drinking hot whiskey and watching old movies. We reminisce about the golden days by the beach, and smile. And I think that no matter where life might have taken me, a small, secret part of me would always have belonged to him.

Comfort

BREDA UNA FORREST

John's father didn't hold out much hope for the calf. "Look, we'll only have to see how it goes. The vet did what he could but it's the shock that's the problem."

"Shock? You mean the fright of it?"

"Ya, that too but physically like. After a big operation like that the body just doesn't know what hit it."

"Oh, right."

"'Tis unfortunate, but that's nature for you. Sure, we've the red lamp over her now so we can only wait and see if she's still around in the morning. We'd better head inside for the supper or your mother'll be after us!" said John's father in higher pitch than normal.

The poor boy was trying his best to be tough. John's mother chatted away, unanswered, while she reheated the supper for him and his father. The younger ones had eaten earlier. John hadn't said a word since he came in from the yard.

"Look Mam, you're not allowed kill me …"

"What have you done?" she interrupted in a voice that'd straighten a bend on the road.

"I'm going to sleep in the calf-house tonight. 499 had a heifer calf there earlier and she had to be operated on, so she's being kept on her own in the pen 'cause of the stitches. I just want to stay with her to make sure she's all right. There's no point telling me not to."

She did anyway.

John continued on with his plan regardless. It was cold out so he brought an old blanket with him. He didn't think he'd need it but it kept his mother quiet (well, quieter). Unbeknown to them, he also hid a bottle of his parents' good whiskey in it.

He had seen his grandfather do it years ago. He put some fresh milk in a tinny bucket and placed it inside a larger bucket of almost boiling water. He kept checking the temperature of the milk with his hand until it was ready. He then poured a couple of capfuls of whiskey into the milk. That didn't seem like enough. This time he poured straight from the bottle into the bucket.

After putting the mixture into a plastic bottle, John knelt down alongside the heifer and he held it to its mouth. She wouldn't drink at first but then she began to take small sups at a time. Halfway through the bottle she stopped. John pulled the blanket over himself and soon they were both asleep in the straw pen.

"God, there's a good bit of life in her eyes this morning. She obviously likes your company John."

"I suppose so," he answered wiping the sleep out of his eyes.

"Hold on! Is that my Powers?"

São Paulo

COLM KEENAN

*H*e wiped the crust off a little pool of Tabasco sauce. All the tables in the restaurant were full, two dozen or so people waiting on the fringes, their eyes shifting back and forth. A boy ran past their table launching a paper airplane. Nearby, a weary-looking waitress was clearing a table, and behind her, two groups were arguing over who got there first. Someone shouted out an order from the swing-doors of the kitchen, the sound amplified in steam.

"What's intelligence?" he asked, unfolding a napkin.

"Intelligence is intelligence."

"Does a virus have intelligence?"

"I don't think so."

"Explain."

"Explain what? They're strands of DNA that can only replicate with a host."

"And is that not a form of intelligence, Iza? Is exploitation not intelligence?"

"Your pizza's getting cold."

Bloated from lunch, they walked hand-in-hand through the swarms of comers and goers in the airport. He bore a sports-bag while she on dainty shoulders carried his backpack. The air was hot. There was a sense of hopelessness in the holding of hands: this day had been coming for two weeks, had been known for two weeks, and every action, every minute gesture, seemed in itself a contradiction, a throwback to the fact.

"Que horas são?" he asked her.

"It's three o' clock."

"We've time yet. What about going to that bookshop over there?"

In the bookshop, they split up. He came across her a few minutes later at the Language section. He liked the way she tilted her head as she read; how she pushed back a strand of black hair behind her multi-pierced ear; the way the heel of her shoe rasped against the carpet unconsciously; how her long fingers turned the page.

They made their way to departures. Families were there gripped in an emotional fission, other couples too. And when they themselves embraced, she broke down, her tears warm as they dripped down the chest of his t-shirt. He lifted her face up to his, and, unsure of what to say, whispered into her ear: "You're special; remember that."

Her body trembled, the tears unceasing. "It's so easy for men. If only you knew how – just go, please, just go!"

The queue through security was in three snake-like lines. She stood where he'd left her with head in hands. The queue moved quickly. He looked for her before going through the door, but she was gone.

Before the metal detector and scanner, he bent forward to undo the belt of his jeans, and it was then that he felt the cool, damp fabric cling to his chest. For the first time in his life, he thought about someone else's journey home.

Dipping Sheep

MIKE McGLADE

*M*y father and I were dipping sheep. To dip sheep requires rhythm. It's a two-man operation and, once we start, there are no breaks until the task is done. With a couple hundred sheep ahead of you, rhythm is what keeps you sane.

You catch and then you pass – it's simple, really. I corner a sheep, sling a rope around its neck, and walk it over to the edge of the dipping trough. Needless to say, sheep don't like to be told what to do, and they'll dig their stumpy little hooves into every crevice possible, will fake a feinting spell, or one will tap me on the shoulder as a distraction, so the other can escape. Sheep are pernickety. A lot of them purposely wear briar necklaces for just such an occasion.

But it's dipping season, and every summer my father and I go through the same rigmarole. Even worse, these sheep are big as bulldozers, fat on summer grass and weighing near as much as me. Thankfully, they haven't yet learned to walk on their hind legs.

My father dips one sheep while I catch another. The dipper stands inside a pit and is slightly above the top of the trough. He plunges the sheep into a wedge-shaped trench, the width of a sheep, which is built into the ground and contains a milky-white liquid that kills parasites. The sheep are in one side of the pen, where I catch them. The only way to get to the other side of the pen is through the dip. The sheep swim along the trench and come out the other end with their eyes squeezed shut, shooting water out of their noses, like a blowhole, before shaking dry like a dog.

The black flies are going crazy in the blistering sun. They'd eat you alive. The dip stops them eating the sheep alive. The milky-white dip looks almost cool and inviting in this heat. We get into a rhythm. Catch-drag-pass-dip. Catch-drag-pass-dip. You forget about everything else. Lost in the moment. I shove the last sheep toward the dipper, pause, and catch my breath. Shouldn't have loitered. Dad catches me, dunks me bodily under the water. I climb out the other end of the dipper, shoot water out of my nose, and shake myself dry like a dog. The sheep cheer.

In hindsight, I probably should have gotten that haircut I had been putting off. I decided to definitely get it cut well in advance of the sheering season.

Dad let the sheep out of the pen, and I joined them on top of Celebration Heath to dry in the sun. Of course, I was blind for a week.

Some serving suggestions
for Powers Whiskey

Hot Powers

- 35.5ml Powers Irish Whiskey
- Boiling Water
- Brown Sugar
- Lemon
- Cloves

METHOD

Pour the Powers into the glass and dissolve the sugar.
Top up with boiling water and stir.
Garnish with a slice of lemon
studded with cloves

Powers Irish Coffee

INGREDIENTS

- 35.5ml Powers Irish Whiskey
- Hot Black Coffee to fill
- Brown Sugar
- Whipped Fresh Cream

METHOD

Pour coffee into the glass and add Powers.
Add one teaspoon of brown sugar and
stir until dissolved. Pour thick cream
over the back of a spoon. The layer
of cream will float on the
coffee without mixing.